ECHOES IN A REFLECTION

PHANTASMAGORIA

SUMEET S. NAVALKAR

Contents

Acknowledgements

I am grateful to all the readers who read this book and gave me their feedback before it was published.

I am grateful to my future readers too for choosing to read this book, and I hope you will not be disappointed.

CHAPTER ONE

Riya:

I am now twenty-four. An old young girl. No, not old but older than when no one expected me to be a mature person. I was born in quite a small village, a few hundred kilometres from the city where I currently live. And I miss that life. Simple. Simple village. Simple life. Simple girl.

I was a studious girl—in school and in college. I read everything that the syllabus prescribed and many other books which the syllabus didn't. A couple of times, the school teachers called my parents and suggested that they admit me to a better school in the city. But I opposed the idea vehemently. My friends, my family—everyone was here. How could I have left them? Well, I was afraid to venture out so far away. Unknown places and unknown people scared me. Here too in the village, I didn't have many friends. Basically, I was a loner who talked less and read about a lot of curious things. And no, not always the seemingly boring stuff. I read fiction too. I was happy being a simple girl who with her two plaits of waist-long hair walked to her school with a bag-load of books.

But then the happy school and college life ended, and for a job, I shifted to the city with my heart in my mouth. My parents stayed with me for a month in the small one-room apartment that we rented in the city. They were my moral support. The small room felt like home because of them. And when I adjusted to the city and my job, my parents returned to our native place. And now, I talk to my parents on the weekends over a video call most of the time. On the weekdays, it's all routine—travelling to work, returning to the room that I call my home now, watching TV sometimes or reading a book and then running back to the office in the morning. Time here in the city passes by as if on the wings of a storm. The hands of a clock, moving fast like the spokes of a wheel.

When I came to the city, given my credentials, it wasn't difficult to procure a job, but adjusting to the people there was a horrendous task. They started making fun of my two plaits. I had styled my hair that way from my childhood and through college, and no one had said anything about it in my village, but here they thought I was weird. Maybe I should have laughed at them too. It's ironic how people can make fun of others when they are in the majority, without thinking logically. The girls here in the city wear high heels which are totally impractical when it comes to walking. I should have laughed at that. They sometimes wear extremely tight skirts—again a walking hazard. They leave their hair untied, an invitation to the city's pollution to get trapped in the locks. They use tissue paper continuously—a waste that harms the environment. And the boys with their ties and coats in the city's hot weather! Not always though. We don't have a strict dress code at our office. But whenever the men have meetings with their managers, they do it. As if the managers would see how they are dressed rather than how they are working. So many illogical things they all do without realising it, and they have the audacity to laugh at my two plaits! But still, they succeeded in making me self-conscious and that too in spite of my being aware that I wasn't doing anything ridiculous. I then started tying my hair in one thick plait. And well, I will admit that it looks good. I am beautiful. No, I am not arrogant about that. I am just stating that as a fact. I am a short, fair-skinned girl with long straight jet-black hair. I am not too thin but on the thinner side. I don't put on any makeup, and I still look beautiful. I dress in traditional wear, nothing showy. Simple—I have always liked it that way. Tying my hair in a single plait instead of two was the only thing I changed or will ever change about myself. No more change ever. I don't care what people think about me. If they don't like me that's their problem, not mine. As it is, I didn't shift to the city to impress anyone or live by their rules.

It's always fun to see my managers appreciating my work over others'. It gives me deep satisfaction to look at their stunned faces. Faces with groomed, shaped moustaches and beards. Faces with shapely thin eyebrows (it makes them look even funnier when they look stunned). Faces with a thick layer of makeup which when it gets mixed with sebum (oil secreted by our skin) after a while looks greasy. Faces with lipstick that extends beyond the lips—how, why, it was always beyond me. And faces with eyeliners above and below the eyes which look like bordered cells on a spreadsheet. I just hate those faces. They look non-human, even inhuman. And expressions of confidence on each face and they walk a cultivated walk to depict the kind of responsibility they are carrying on their shoulders. As if the smooth working of the office is only because of their fake confidence, their gait, their expression, their beards and their makeup. And then when I am appreciated over them... That's when I see the clowns beneath the masked faces.

That 'I don't care' attitude that I cultivated after coming into the city, I have liked it. People's gossip, their expressions when they look at me, they don't affect me any longer. And I like it when they know their taunts have no effect on me. But this carefree attitude of mine does not always work—at least not in all situations. In fact, it works well except in one special situation. That day, I saw him near the water cooler. His name is Jay. It's not that it was the first time that I saw him that day. I had seen him quite a number of times before but I had remained unaffected by him. But that day, I saw him up close. I had never been attracted to him before because I never felt he was attractive. He was OK but not that attractive. But that day when I saw him, my opinion about him completely changed. He was indeed handsome. I was surprised because usually, the opposite happens with most of us. We might look at a person from a distance and feel he is attractive but when we go and talk to the person and see him up close, we see the flaws in his looks, and we may end up feeling that the person is not as good-looking as we thought. But with Jay, the exact opposite happened. Up close, he looked totally handsome. I blushed and averted my eyes from him. He filled up his bottle and left.

In the following days, I started observing him. He used to go to lunch at around noon, and then he used to come back from the canteen and fill up his bottle at around 12:30 PM. I then started filling up my bottle too at the same time. That way, I got to be near him, and I liked the feeling. I knew I was attracted to him. That was surprising. I never had this feeling for anyone in my school or even college days. This was the first time that I felt like this. Butterflies in my stomach. And the butterflies perhaps reproduced each day, because the intensity of this feeling increased with each passing day. And one day, I finally opened my mouth.

"Hi," I said.

He looked up.

"Hi," he acknowledged my greeting.

"Our times match," I said. "I see you almost every day here."

"Yes, maybe I have seen you too, I think."

He *had* noticed me. He *has* noticed me, my mind cried out in joy. But I didn't let it show on my face.

"Bye," Jay said and left.

The next day, I went a bit early to fill up my bottle. I didn't want him to think, or rather know, that I go there at the same time to interact with him. I was hoping I wasn't too early. But I wasn't. Just as my bottle filled up, he came. I smiled, and he looked confused.

"It's me... fr-from ye-yesterday..," I stammered.

"Oh yes. Sorry. Hi."

But hadn't he said yesterday that he too had noticed me before? Then how could he forget that I talked to him yesterday?

"Hi," I replied.

For a moment, I hesitated, not able to decide whether to say anything more or not. But then I left.

For the next two days, I did not go to the water cooler at 12:30 PM. Maybe he would notice my absence, I thought. But in addition to that, I also didn't want to come face-to-face with him. What if he failed to recognise me again? I realised that I had been thinking a lot about him lately. I wanted him to be attracted to me the same way I was attracted to him. But why, especially when we were not even friends? Friends? We didn't even know each other's names at the time. On the third day, I went to the cooler. He was already there. He looked up at me and nodded. He recognised me.

"You recognised me?" I blurted out without thinking.

"Oh. I am sorry about that day. I am bad at remembering names and faces. By the way, I am Jay," he said and extended his right hand.

I felt numb as I held his hand.

"I am Neet... oh sorry, Riya."

Oh, what is wrong with me? How can I not say *my* name correctly?

"What?" Jay exclaimed and laughed.

"What?" I said, faking annoyance. "Only you can be bad at remembering names and faces?"

"Oh. You were taunting me?" He said and smiled. "That was a good one."

He was impressed, wasn't he? He must have thought I was witty. Good that I forgot my own name.

The next day, I walked to the cooler a bit early and hoped Jay would come before my bottle filled up.

"Hi Riya," he said, and I missed a heartbeat.

"Jay, isn't that what your name is?" I said, smiling mischievously at him.

"Yes. OK. Revenge, huh?"

My bottle filled up, but I stayed there till he filled up his bottle. And then we walked together till our paths diverged to our respective places.

Day after day, the words, Riya, Jay, hi and bye fell on the heap of our earlier conversations, which also contained those exact same words. I wasn't making any progress. I so desperately wanted to have a real conversation with him, but I didn't know what to say. But then couldn't he try it from his side?

In retrospect, I think—how crazy I was to have thought of wooing Jay? I hadn't known the outcome then. Otherwise, I wouldn't have tried. But getting attracted to him wasn't in my hands. Now it's over. It's over. Get over it. This is what I try to tell myself as I sit on the barricade separating the sea from the land. This is a coastal city. And for the past ten days after that fateful day, I have been coming here day after office hours and am trying to get over him. But I feel depressed, rejected. It's over, but still not over for me.

"Hi," I heard a voice from somewhere behind me.

I turned to my left. I didn't see her. Then I turned right. She was a short girl, about my age. Hair short, cut like a boy's.

"May I sit here?" she asked politely.

This was the barricade I was sitting on, with boulders between it and the sea, to stop the waves from striking the wall directly. The place wasn't very crowded. Then why did she want to sit here beside me? I wanted to say that but didn't.

"This is a public place. You can sit wherever you wish to," I said instead.

CHAPTER TWO

Jay:

This girl in my office, Riya. We happened to first meet at the water cooler. And our conversations were mostly made up of salutations. We greeted each other. But there were times when she talked and I found her witty. And yes, she is beautiful. Initially, I hadn't noticed her, but later I realised how beautiful she was. She was low profile but definitely beautiful. I hadn't thought about her romantically. But then one day, instead of her usual acknowledgement of my presence, she said something surprising.

"I come here at this perfect time just to talk to you," she was quite straightforward. "Do you think, sometime we could go out?"

I was surprised. But I liked it. I could not have said no. As I said, she is beautiful. And witty.

"Yes. OK. When?" I asked.

"Tonight?"

"Yes. That's fine with me," I replied.

And so that day, we met later in the evening, away from her and my home and away from the office as well. We had dinner at a quiet place. And then we strolled along the sea. The coastline is long and extends for the entire north-south length of the city. We talked about our lives. Mostly hers. I had the usual boring childhood of a city boy, and there was nothing to talk about that. Her story, on the contrary, was interesting. At least, I felt so. The simplicity of the village life felt attractive coming from her sweet voice and expressive eyes. And yes, my initial impression about her being witty was proved correct—she had always been a top-ranker at school and college.

After a while, she said it was getting late. And a thought crossed my mind. What if she called me to her place for the night? Unlike me who stayed with my family, she stayed alone. Would I go with her if she called? How would I not? She's beautiful. But what would I say to my family? Such sudden plans would create suspicion. A night with a girl meant only one thing, and anyone could guess. I couldn't have lied about going out with my friends. Such excursions were always well-planned, and my family knew it. What then? At that moment, Riya hailed a taxi.

"We will meet again. Won't we?" she said, smiling one of her sweetest smiles.

"Yes."

And then I don't know what got into me. I pulled her towards me and kissed her on her lips. Then thinking, she would hate me for that, I released her quickly and looked nervously at her for her reaction. She looked surprised. She turned away, opened the door of the taxi but then stopped, looked back at me, stood on her toes and kissed me back. Then she smiled and left without a word.

A few minutes later, reality sank in. I had kissed Riya. Accepting her proposal to go out that night was itself an indication to her that I could be interested in her. But to actually kiss her on our first day out, indicated a lot more seriousness. I shouldn't have kissed her. I should have taken it slowly, kept my options open. I needed my options open, not because I found anything unacceptable about Riya but because of this girl, Beena. She also works at my office, and I had been trying to seek her attention for a while. She had given me mixed signals, and I felt confused about asking her out. I am not as straightforward as Riya. She was interested in me, and she asked me. I, on the other hand, couldn't do the same with Beena. Beena made me nervous. And meanwhile, Riya asked me, consequently tempting me. But Riya wasn't my first preference.

The next day, I decided I would have to talk to Beena. Almost always, she was the only one I had for company when I went to have my lunch at noon.

"I went on a date yesterday," I said as casually as I could, halfway through our lunch.

She looked up, surprised. But the next moment, she recovered, her face unreadable.

"Good for you," she said indifferently.

Now that struck me as fake. Her indifference was fake. We were friends. Very good friends, in fact. A friend would have definitely asked with whom I had gone on a date. Her efforts to show that she was unaffected gave her away. And I decided to take advantage of it.

"Yes, definitely good," I said. "In fact, we have decided to meet again. She stays alone in this city, and I am hoping she invites me over to her place after the dinner."

Beena's expression changed.

"You all are the same. All you want is sex."

"What's wrong with doing something that concerns no one else and gives two people pleasure?"

CHAPTER THREE

Beena:

I have always liked Jay. But I didn't want to commit. And that's because I am not sure if I want to be with him all my life. We have a good rapport, but then how can I be sure that it will last forever? My friends tell me that I can never be sure and that if I stick to this attitude of mine, I will lose all prospective partners. But still, it's scary to commit. But Jay came and told me he had gone on a date. I initially expressed indifference. That has always been my instinct whenever he has alluded to anything romantic. But as I absorbed the news, I realised I might lose him to someone. Should I lose him? Maybe the next man I am attracted to will be better than Jay. Jay told me he was hoping his date would invite him to her place. That meant nothing had happened between the last night. And who was this girl who he had suddenly got interested in?

"But where did you find her? Who is this girl?" I asked him, still not finding myself being frank with him.

He shifted in his chair, looking uncomfortable.

"Ummm... You know her."

"Is she from here? Our office?"

"Yes. Riya."

"Riya? Who's Riya? Oh, don't tell me it's the one with two plaits."

"Well, yes. That Riya. But now she is just one-plaited Riya."

I was now literally shocked. Losing Jay to someone else would have been acceptable but to that two-plaited weird girl! Jay, how could you? Don't you have any class?

"Don't you have any class?" I blurted it out without thinking.

"You are jealous. Tell me you are," he said something like this for the first time, something which didn't just suggest a connection between us, but was a direct statement.

And no, I could not have lost him to Riya.

"Yes, jealous," I admitted. "But more shocked than jealous."

"Jealous is good. Does it mean you will go out with me?"

"And what about her?" I couldn't even say her name, and I said what I said to him with a tone and expression which must have only meant disgust.

But it wasn't intentional. It was just a reaction to the shock.

"I will go and tell her that I cannot go out with her anymore," he replied.

"Are you sure?"

"Are you sure you will go out with me?" he answered with a question.

He was asking for commitment. Well, almost. My mind squirmed at the thought of commitment. But I liked him and couldn't lose him for someone like her.

"Yes, I will go out with you."

"Not just once."

"OK. Not just once or twice but more."

"If I had known you would be jealous and go out with me, I would have gone out with Riya much earlier," he said and smiled.

I couldn't help smiling back.

CHAPTER FOUR

Jay:

I had to tell Riya. It was going to be difficult. I shouldn't have kissed her. That suggested we would go out again. I felt a bit guilty. But I had no option but to tell her frankly. Waiting at the water cooler, I was going over how I would tell her when Riya came and looking at me, smiled. She looked happy. And I was going to ruin her mood.

"Riya...," I said tentatively.

"Jay," she smiled.

"I need to tell you that I can no longer go out with you."

Riya's smile disappeared. She just stood there without saying anything. And I didn't know what to say.

"I am sorry," I said, mostly in search of a response.

"It's OK," she said finally. "But can you tell me frankly what happened?"

And I told her about how I had liked Beena for a long time. I also told her about the conversation I had with Beena. I told Riya that going out with her had actually helped me with Beena's case.

"So I was the trigger?" Riya said. "And what did she say about me?"

"Beena felt bad about you," I lied.

"Liar. You want me to believe that Beena felt bad about the two-plaited weird girl?"

I was stunned. How could Riya possibly know what Beena said to me? And my face must have said it.

"There were so many people who said things about me. And Beena was one of them," she explained. "And I know what they call me."

I didn't say a word.

"Bye," she said and started to leave without filling up her bottle.

"I am sorry," I said.

She turned, faced me.

"Jay, I am quite sure that Beena accepted to go out with you only because I was the girl you went out with. If it had been someone else other than me, Beena may not have agreed to go out with you. Are you sure you want to be with someone like her?"

"Why do you think so?" I asked, not able to understand her logic.

"Female psychology. She could have lost you to someone else probably. But she couldn't lose you to me. What would people think? That Beena's best friend is going out with the girl that Beena finds disgusting. They would laugh at you and in turn at her because you are best friends."

But I still wanted to go out with Beena. Riya stood there for a couple of moments, perhaps hoping I would be convinced. But I didn't say anything. She then turned and left.

CHAPTER FIVE

Riya:

Ten days had passed by since Jay told me that he was not going out with me. He doesn't understand how much I like him. I didn't show it to him, but since that day I first saw him at the water cooler, I have been unable to drive him out of my mind. And now this rejection. Rejection comes with obsession. Am I obsessed with him? Maybe but who cares? For the last ten days, I have been here, looking at the sea and the beautiful sunset. But that hasn't soothed my mind a bit, and now this girl disturbed me and interrupted my thoughts about Jay. She was polite, asking me if she could sit here, but I feel it's rude to invade someone's space when there is so much free place here on the barricade. She came and just sat there, a few inches to my right. A few minutes have passed. She hasn't said anything. I feel like getting up and leaving. But if I do it, I may be rude to her. And what about my ego? How would I feel later? That a stranger disturbed me and I left when I didn't want to.

"I have been seeing you here for the last week or so," she said, interrupting my train of thought.

"Yes, I have been here."

"Hmmm... Alone. No one else."

"Yes. Alone. Aren't you alone too?" I asked.

"Yes. Alone. But I am always like that. Loner."

"Me too. Loner."

"Oh. Good. We can become friends," she said, sounding a tad excited.

"Just because we are loners, we can become friends! Wouldn't that change us to non-loners?"

"Yes. That would. And then because we both turn into non-loners, we can become friends again."

I just looked at her.

"Oh. Come on. I am just kidding," she said. "Saying something to make a conversation. I came and sat here because since I noticed you some days back, I had a feeling that you might be upset about something."

"And what if it's true?" I asked a bit bluntly.

"You can share your problems with me."

"What? Why would I share anything with you? Why would I share anything with a stranger?"

"Exactly. A stranger. Spilling your mind out with a stranger is easier. See, I don't know your friends. You don't know mine. I don't know your family. You don't know mine. Whatever you share with me stays with me, at least practically. I cannot share it with anyone you know because I don't know them. Moreover, you need not even worry about me judging you. I am a stranger. If I don't like you, we don't meet and you can have all the hard feelings for me. I won't even know."

I squinted at her. Logical, I thought. She had a point.

"Am I convincing?" she asked.

"Maybe."

She smiled.

"My name is Priya," she said.

"Wow. Riya with a P," I mumbled.

"What? I didn't catch that."

"I am Riya," I said.

"Oh. Similar sounding names, we have," she said and extended her hand to shake mine.

I extended my hand. She shook it but released it after two long moments.

"Now that we know each other's names, are we still strangers?" I asked.

She smiled but said nothing. I returned her smile. A smile costs nothing.

CHAPTER SIX

Priya:

I had watched Riya for ten days before I approached her. I didn't know how to. I saw this simple, beautiful girl sitting all by herself, looking at the sea and looking upset. Well, I am a loner too, but I know when someone is sad. Seeing Riya there made me feel something was wrong. I didn't want to encroach on her space. So I had refrained from going and talking to her. But day after day, she came and just sat there with a blank expression. It was as if she was writing a book, page after page, but all the pages blank because the ink in her pen had dried up. I wanted to be her outlet—to make her drain out all her pent-up emotions. Why? Because I felt for her. It didn't feel right to just watch a seemingly nice girl, looking blankly at the setting sun, her gaze blank yet intense as if she could bore a hole through the sun. She sat there with nothing but only her sorrow for company. The sorrow, which had perhaps turned to stone in her mind. I wanted to melt it so that it could flow out of her mind and release her, free her of her pain. And the blank pages of her life's book could fill up again.

Riya is a reluctant speaker. And I can understand that. I am one too. She didn't want to share her pain. The day after I talked to her, I saw her again. I had wanted to see her again—I felt drawn towards her. But I had also hoped that she would get on with her life, forgetting whatever sorrow that was nibbling at her mind even if that meant she stopped coming here. However, I was glad to see her. Firstly because she did come back even though she knew she could run into me again. Secondly, because I at least knew she was safe in the sense that she was alive; people go to any extent in depression. I decided to wait for a few minutes because I felt she wouldn't appreciate my presence so soon. But those minutes turned into half an hour. I didn't have the courage to go and meet her. What if she was rude to me? I wouldn't like that. Moreover, she just sat there; she didn't look around to check if I was there. She did not want me. Yes, maybe that was the truth that I needed her more than she needed me. Why would I think this way? What did I need from her? Maybe it made me feel important when someone took my help and was grateful for it. Everything is selfish, isn't it? Everything—including social service. A social worker gives service to society, and let me tell you, there is nothing selfless about that. He does it because it gives him a high. It makes him feel important—a change that he is able to bring about in someone's life. A social worker may donate money to the poor. Now someone may say that this act is selfless, and there is nothing that he gains from it. But no. There is always something to gain. He may donate because he cannot bear to see the plight of the poor. And if he does not donate, he feels guilty about it—that he can make someone's life better and yet he is not helping. So to avoid feeling guilty, he donates. That's how the act becomes selfish. He may donate and become poor himself. But he does so because he would prefer to be poor himself rather than watch someone else suffer. His preferences may be different than most people, but that does not make him selfless. He makes a choice that is more satisfying to him. That's selfish. Everything is selfish. My sympathy for Riya is selfish. My wanting to help her is selfish. Good deeds do happen because of selfishness. Being selfish to a point where you don't hurt anyone else is not wrong. It's good. These thoughts gave me courage. And I got up and started walking towards where Riya was sitting.

I stood behind her.

"Hi Riya," I said softly.

CHAPTER SEVEN

Riya:

I turned to my left. I didn't see her. Then I turned right and there she was.

"Hi Priya," I said.

I was rather glad to see her. I don't know exactly why though. Maybe her showing interest in me flattered my ego. Perhaps it made me feel that I wasn't as small as this city had always made me feel. At least for her, I was important, and somewhere deep down, it was satisfying. I shifted a bit to make space for her. And that was absolutely unnecessary because there was no one else around. But that was a gesture which Priya understood, and she sat down beside me on my right.

We watched the sea for several minutes. Every wave, rushing towards us, breaking on the boulders, splashing drops which sometimes reached us, then receding, again to come back strongly. Inanimate nature also tells a story as if it has a life of its own.

"Why do you want me to share my story? Why do you want to help?" I asked Priya.

"Hidden agenda," she replied and I chuckled.

"The sun's almost down. I need to go home," I said.

"And I thought you were just opening up. That's fine though. Some other time whenever you want to."

"Tomorrow?" I said that without thinking, almost admitting to her and to myself that I would like to see her again.

"Yes, I will be here."

"Are you always here?"

"Yes. I work nearby and after office hours, I like to linger."

I shook her hand as I stood up to leave, and like the day before, she held my hand a moment longer.

I was avoiding crossing paths with Jay since that day, and I was successful the next day too. After office, I went and sat down at my usual spot on the barricade wall. I looked around for Priya but didn't see her. I kept looking intermittently for a few minutes but couldn't spot her anywhere. Maybe she was stuck up at work. I sighed. For once, I had thought about sharing my pain with someone, but maybe I wasn't destined to. Thinking she wouldn't come today, I watched the sea and its waves and tried to listen to the soothing sound of water to distract myself.

"Hi Riya," Priya said softly from somewhere behind me.

This time, I turned right and I saw her. I tapped on the concrete of the barricade, inviting her to sit.

"I looked for you when I reached her," I said.

"Nice to know that," Priya said and smiled. "So? Was your day better today?"

"No."

"Want to tell me what's happening in your life?"

"Maybe. But don't you have other friends who are waiting for you?"

"*Other* friends? Does that mean the two of us are friends now?" She caught me in words.

"Maybe," I replied.

"No, no one's waiting for me. As I told you, I am a loner."

"Yes, you told me that. Well about my life... It happened a few days back," I said, not knowing how to begin. "I am infatuated with someone at my office."

"A boy?" she asked.

I looked at her, a bit confused.

"Yes, who else?" I said.

"I meant a boy or a man?"

"Oh no. He's my age."

"OK. So, what happened?" she asked and I told her the entire story which started at the water cooler, made a detour with a date and ended again at the water cooler.

Priya remained silent for a few minutes, reflecting on the story, watching the waves rise and ebb. I looked at her as she watched the sea. Her chest rose and fell as she breathed, the same way the waves rose and receded. The ocean breathes too, I thought; the water is the blood and the waves the result of a giant heartbeat.

"So Beena basically snatched Jay away from you," she said.

"Yes, she did. But that does not make Jay innocent, does it?"

"No, it doesn't," she agreed, turned to me and touched my cheek. "They are both responsible for hurting my friend here."

That gesture welled up my eyes, but I controlled my emotions and looked away towards the sea and the now-setting sun.

Priya and I continued to meet daily. We didn't discuss anything about the office, Jay or Beena. I never asked her about her office; she never told me anything. I didn't tell her about my office or the work I do either. We didn't need to know. At least I didn't need to. We were just content being there, being there with each other. We didn't even know where the other stayed. We didn't exchange phone numbers. Perhaps we both thought our friendship might be short-lived or perhaps our friendship didn't need any of the unwritten norms that society imposes. We were content meeting each other and watching the sea and the sunset. That didn't however mean that we didn't talk. Yes, we didn't chat continuously but we talked about movies, places, seas, countries, science, geography and whatnot. I was surprised that she could talk on all the subjects I usually found difficult talking with others. We were similar. And yet, we didn't share our phone numbers. Perhaps I am to blame for this. All good things come to an end someday like what happened with Jay, and so I wanted some sort of detachment in this newly-found attachment with Priya. And I was glad she was very understanding, and she never brought up any personal information during our talks.

Then one day, Priya brought up the subject again.

"How are you holding up, Riya?" she asked.

"Frankly, I am still disturbed. Jay doesn't seem to be leaving my thoughts so soon," I said, and automatically, my body became stiff. She noticed it as her eyes fell on my stiffened neck muscles. She patted my head gently and stood up.

"You know why I always sit at your right?" she asked.

I had never noticed that. But now that she asked, I realised that it had indeed always been so.

"No. Why?"

"Because I am your right-hand man," she said and walked and stood exactly behind me. "I will be there when you need me."

"Yes, I think I know that, and I am grateful to you for that," I said without looking back at her.

Priya placed her hands on my shoulders and held them gently but firmly. My shoulder muscles relaxed. She then moved her fingers to my neck and coaxed my stiff muscles to relax. I relaxed them. That was the first time I noticed how many muscles in our body stiffen when we think about something unpleasant. And I had been thinking about unpleasant things for so many days. She moved her fingers from my neck to my shoulders and back to my neck again, massaging the muscles gently, slowly. She repeated it a number of times. It felt good, relaxing. I closed my eyes and breathed deeply trying to empty my mind of all thoughts. She brought her hands back to my neck and paused. Then her fingers slid slightly below my clavicles, inching very slowly down my chest. At first, it felt relaxing and then a slight sensual tingling feeling coursed through my body, tightening my muscles again. Her hands touched my bare skin above my breasts. And then I realised she was Priya—a girl. I suddenly became uncomfortable. I held her hands, stopping them from sliding further down and opened my eyes and turned to look at her. She removed her hands quickly away and avoided looking at me. Slowly, tentatively, she came and sat beside me again. I remained silent; I didn't know what to say. I too avoided looking at her now. It was awkward. But I needed to say something, to ask her something. I had to know.

"Are you…," I said but couldn't complete my question.

Priya looked straight towards the sea, unable to say anything. It must be awkward for her too, I thought.

"If you are feeling embarrassed, please don't," I said. "Just tell me. Are you homosexual?"

"It's called lesbian," she said, not quite answering my question.

"I am just using the scientific term. Tell me, are you a homosexual?"

"Yes," she admitted and looked down at her feet dangling from the barricade.

"OK," I could only think of saying that. "OK, but… Then… OK. Now I see. You had asked me whether my crush was a boy. You were trying to find out if I was a heterosexual or a homosexual. Then again when I asked you why you were helping me, you said you had a hidden agenda. Believe me, I am not judging you, but when you said you had an agenda, was it to seduce me? Again, I am just asking, not judging."

"I wanted to help you, really. Believe me if you can. But yes, I was drawn to you. Maybe my subconscious wanted to try and seduce you. And at the moment, it's not that simple. It's no longer remained just sexual or physical attraction. I think I have started liking… loving you."

"Oh no. Don't. I respect your feelings for me. I do. But I won't be able to reciprocate them—ever. I am heterosexual. Straight, if you will."

"Yes, I got that now. I am sorry."

"It's OK," I said.

"It's OK?" she said incredulously. "I just made a pass at you and it's OK?"

"Yes, it's fine. I said I respect your feelings. I just can't reciprocate them. Do you believe me?"

"OK. Yes, I do. Thanks. But now what? Hasn't our friendship just become complicated?"

"Yes, it has," I sighed. What else could I say?

"So you won't be meeting me tomorrow onwards?"

"I didn't say that," I said, not knowing where our friendship would now go after she admitted to having feelings for me.

And I didn't know how this worked. I had never known any homosexual person in my life. I felt confused. I just didn't know what to do. But I didn't want to hurt her either. I got up.

"I will be leaving now. See you tomorrow," I said.

"Really?" Priya was surprised.

"Yes."

I extended my hand to shake and at that moment, I realised why Priya's hand had always lingered on mine. But this time, she shook my hand and quickly released it.

The next day, we met as usual. But both of us seemed to have nothing to say. She kept looking at the sea the way I had before I first met her.

"Nothing to say?" I asked her.

"I am upset."

"Why?"

"Why were you upset when Jay couldn't reciprocate your feelings?"

"OK. Got it. Sorry."

Silence again. A long awkward time later, just as the sun was about to set, Priya looked at me.

"I am your right-hand man," she said.

"Huh?" I didn't know what she meant.

"How are you?" she asked.

I raised my eyebrows, confused. I didn't know where this conversation was leading.

"I am asking you with regards to Jay and Beena."

"Oh. Perhaps you and I are sailing in the same boat."

"Still not good, that means. Right?" "It's better than it was at the start. But yes, you are right. Not good. I keep thinking about him. I avoid coming face to face with him. It pains when I see Jay and Beena together."

"I wanted to see them," she said. "Just wanted to see how he looks and what he saw in Beena. Do you have their photos?"

"No," I replied. "No, wait. I might. There was this group photo that someone sent me on chat."

I went through my phone and found it.

"Here," I said. "That's Jay and she is Beena."

"She's sexy," Priya said after she wolf-whistled.

My face fell. She looked at me and smiled.

"Yes, she's sexy," Priya repeated. "But that does not mean she is sexier than you."

And that made me blush and extremely self-conscious. Priya laughed, looking at me, not at all feeling awkward.

"You know," she said, "why you are still in bad shape? Because you haven't got a closure."

"I don't know how I will get one. But what about you? How will you get yours?"

"I will get it when you get yours. You see I wouldn't have met you if you hadn't been depressed. You were depressed because of Jay and Beena. So when you get your closure, I will get mine."

I did not understand the logic.

"But how will I get mine?" I asked, ignoring the question I had about what she just said.

"It's all psychological."

"Meaning?" I asked.

But Priya didn't answer. She got up to leave.

"I may or may not see you for the next few days. I may not have time to come here. Some work has come up. But if you come here every day, chances are we might meet someday. But don't wait for me. If you get your closure and stop coming, this is a final bye."

"What? No. If I stop coming here daily, I will still come here every Wednesday and wait till the sunset."

"Done. I will look for you on Wednesdays if I happen to be around."

"But we can stay in touch through…"

"No. It's better this way."

"Yes. In fact, I agree with you."

Priya gestured for me to stand up. I did. And she hugged me. A tight long hug. Our bodies pressed against each other's. I hugged her back though I was a bit uncomfortable, but Priya didn't feel the awkwardness.

"I would have kissed you now on your lips, had you been a lesbian," she said and my eyes widened.

Priya laughed and waved a bye. I waved back. That was quite moody of her. She said she was upset when we met. Then all of a sudden, her mood became light and she left quite abruptly. Moreover, it felt like she had decided not to meet me again. Different people react differently to stress. Maybe staying away from me—the root cause of her stress—was the choice she opted for. I also wished good for her. So, it was fine with me if staying away from me helped her. Priya was always an enigma. Trying to rescue me from my emotions, becoming a friend, trying to seduce me, falling in love with me—all this was totally unexpected. Priya, I will miss you.

CHAPTER EIGHT

Priya:

The first time I saw Riya, I was attracted to her. No, I did not befriend her to seduce her or to woo her. Falling for her happened unknowingly even when I knew she was straight. Yes, I did hope her sexual orientation may change because of me, for me. But unfortunately, it didn't. But I always felt protective about her... That was instinctive. I couldn't protect her from what had already happened in her life before I met her. But that should not prevent me from giving her the closure that she needed. I loved Riya and she gave me a new objective.

It was Monday when I told Riya we might not meet again. But when Wednesday came, I went to the barricade near the sea. I didn't meet her. She did not see me because she wasn't expecting me to be there on the very first Wednesday. I kept my distance and watched her watching the sea. And I left when she left. I missed her, and this was the least I could do to be with her and give my eyes the pleasure of seeing her. But there was work to do. After I had left on Monday, since that time, I had been scanning social networking sites in search of Jay and Beena. If I found one of them, I would find the other. Finally I found them both on Thursday on two different sites. They had photos with each other and the latest updates showed what places they usually visited. There was this bar that they both visited intermittently, perhaps on the weekends. I had to be there.

On Friday, I went to the bar at around 5:30 PM. I ordered an alcoholic beverage and sat down at a table, keeping my eyes open for Jay and Beena. I kept looking at the door to the entrance for about an hour. Every time the door opened, I scanned the entrants. But I didn't see Jay and Beena. I ordered another drink and swallowed half of it in a gulp. I stood up. Alcohol acts as a diuretic, and my bladder was full. I didn't know where the washroom was. Before asking anyone, I looked around. And at the end of the hall, I saw them. Jay! And beside him, Beena. I forgot about the pressure on my bladder. Now what?—I thought. Should I go there? I had no plan. I mean I knew my goal but I had no plan of how to reach it—how to approach them when I saw them. There was no use having a plan for that because I didn't know under what conditions, I was going to see them. But whatever plan I had, was it to be executed today? Most probably, yes. I didn't know when I would see them again. And I had no information on what other places they visited regularly. My lips suddenly went dry as I took a step towards them. But then suddenly, Beena stood up. Jay stood up too and let Beena leave the table. Then he sat down again as Beena started walking in my direction. Wow, that was convenient, I thought. I moved my hand through my short hair and flattened it further. I buttoned up my jacket, realised I had my earrings still on, removed them quickly and slid them into my pant pockets. Then I put on my tinted glasses and clenched my jaw. I hoped all this would work. It should, I said to myself. It was still quite early and the bar was quite not full. Moreover, there were fewer women compared to the men. I had been a fool to assume that I would reach early and wait for them. They were here before me. Beena directly approached me. A couple of metres away from me, she took a sharp left. Well, it looked sharp because she was drunk, I suppose. She tried to walk straight and she did, but the turn gave her drunken state away. I followed her, assuming she was going to the washroom. She opened the door to the washroom. As I followed, a waiter stopped me.

"Sorry sir," he said to me. "The gents washroom is to the right."

I looked at him sharply.

"Oh sorry, madam. I'm extremely sorry."

"It's OK," I said, actually feeling bad for him.

If a sober waiter was fooled then... I went inside the washroom. I couldn't see Beena. I went into one of the cubicles and quickly urinated, flushed and came out, washed my hands and waited in a corner. A few seconds later, I heard a flushing sound. Beena stepped out of one of the cubicles. There was no one else there, and she must have thought she was alone. She didn't even try to walk straight. She opened the tap of the wash basin. I quietly approached her.

"Hey babe!" I whispered.

Whispers don't have gender. A whisper from a male sounds the same as from a female. Beena turned in my direction. She was startled, and she turned so quickly that she teetered and lost her balance. She would have fallen down, had I not held her wrist firmly and pulled her.

"Oh. Thanks," she said. "Firm grip."

She smiled sheepishly.

"You almost scared me," she said. "Oops. Did I enter the men's room?"

"Does it matter?" I said in a husky voice.

"I should get out quickly."

"No need. No one's here."

Beena looked at me. But I noticed her eyes couldn't focus properly because of the alcohol. She kept blinking. She perhaps suspected that I was a woman or perhaps that I was a man who had entered the ladies washroom.

"Checking me out?" I asked.

She smiled.

"No. No."

"You can if you want to. Because I am checking you out. You are hot," I said.

Beena giggled.

"It's inappropriate of you to say that. I am here with my boyfriend."

"There is no one here except for you and me," I informed her.

"But I have a boyfriend."

"Lucky lad."

"Yes, lucky, he is."

"And he can continue to *think* he is lucky."

"You're suggesting something? Because if you are, I am still not interested."

"I can say you are indeed interested," I said, moving a little closer to her. "You should always keep your options open. You don't know when you will find someone more perfect for you."

"Oh. You think like me," she said.

Alcohol induces frankness.

"Hmmm... Commitment traps you." I was trying her own philosophy on her.

Riya had told me about Jay and Beena's conversation. Both Riya and I had concluded that Beena, by nature, must have always avoided commitment. Otherwise, she would have already been his girlfriend. When she thought she might lose Jay to Riya, only then she hastily agreed to go out with him and be his girlfriend. It was claiming Jay for herself. She wanted Jay but only if she couldn't find anyone better. But now, I was standing in front of her and telling her she had an option and that her boyfriend need not know about it. Would she take it, especially when she was drunk?

She teetered towards me. I grasped her hand and gently pulled her close to me. Our bodies collided. I put my left arm around her waist, not letting her push herself away from me. Then I looked into her eyes. She stared back with her eyes still unable to focus. But I am good-looking, and she must have thought me to be handsome. With my right hand, I touched and caressed her neck. And then quickly kissed her lips. She gasped but only out of surprise. Alcohol had freed her of some of her inhibitions.

"That was soft. Nice...," she said.

I pulled her even closer and kissed her again—this time passionately but gently. And she kissed me back.

"Soft. Sensual," she whispered and resumed kissing.

After a few seconds, I pushed her away.

"Let's go to your apartment or mine," I suggested.

"But..."

"Message your boyfriend that you left. Had too much alcohol."

"Will he believe me?"

"Why not? You *are* drunk."

"So am I making the right decision?"

"Right or wrong is only when others find out about it."

"I agree. You think so much like me," she said and brought her phone out, unlocked it with a pin which I recorded in my memory.

In the next couple of minutes, we were out of the bar after I paid my bill with two more beer cans included in the final amount. We got a taxi, and she said she would take me to her apartment, which was convenient for me. I made her drink a beer in the taxi itself. She was happy gulping it down quickly.

Beena was full of passion. As soon as she closed the door of her apartment, she threw her bag on the sofa and started kissing me on my lips. Yes, she was sexy.

"Let's get to a bed first," I protested from between the kisses.

"Yes. Right," she agreed and teetered towards her bedroom.

I quickly went to the sofa and got her phone out of her bag, unlocked it with the pin from my memory, replaced the bag on the sofa and followed her to the bedroom. Meanwhile, I opened the camera app on her phone and started recording a video using the front camera.

By the time, I was able to place her phone on the desk by her bed, Beena was already lying on her bed, yearning for me to come and join her. I bent down on top of her and kissed her, making sure her face was visible on the phone's screen.

"What's your name? I didn't even ask," she said.

"Does it matter?"

"No, it doesn't."

I kissed her again, and she kissed me back passionately. I then sat up on top of her and told her to close her eyes. She did. I quickly fetched her phone, stopped the recording, clicked on share and sent the video to Jay. And then I started the recording again. I held both her hands and slowly brought them towards my breasts. I no longer cared if she found out that I was a girl. My work was done. She gasped.

"You're a girl!" she said in a stunned voice.

"Yes."

"That's why you were so gentle, so soft. Oh please, finish off what you started," she said, fondling with my breasts, her body squirming in anticipation of pleasure.

Now it was my turn to be stunned. This was totally unexpected.

"You are a bisexual?"

"No. But I am loving this."

"Maybe that's because you are drunk. And you may regret this in the morning."

"Regret is only if someone else finds out," she paraphrased what I had told earlier at the bar.

Is it so, I thought, then you are so going to regret this. I stopped the recording. There was now one more recording to be sent. What happened next could not be recorded though. It was too private.

We had both undressed. I rode her. Without much alcohol in my body, I still felt inebriated. I moved my hands on her forearms. They were smooth, hairless, waxed, soft. And I became conscious of the vellus hair on my arms and legs. I never waxed my body. I believed in being natural. I looked at her face for any change in expression as she too moved her hands on my arms. She didn't seem to mind at all. The hair was short and soft, but I still wondered what if it turned her off. But nothing changed. My hands proceeded moving up her arms towards her shoulders and then down towards her breasts. She mimicked my actions. It was like our sensory systems had become one. My brain seemed to control her actions and her brain mine. Pleasure flowed freely between our bodies. If only this hadn't been one-time, I thought. If only we had met under different circumstances. If only I could have a relationship with her. But no, Beena had hurt Riya. But whatever it was, I was going to go home the next morning with good memories of the night.

CHAPTER NINE

Beena:

My head was spinning when I got up in the morning. It took me a few moments to remember what had happened the night before and during the night. Thinking of her, I again felt aroused. And then I looked around. No one else seemed to be in my apartment except me. Was all that a dream? Maybe it was. I am straight. How would I get sexually attracted to a girl? But had she not hidden it from me? But was she real or a figment of my imagination? I turned on my side and suddenly inhaled a whiff of a perfume that wasn't mine. That fragrance reminded me of her. She was real indeed. What was her name? Did she tell me? What was her phone number? I lifted myself on my elbows and looked at the side table. There was no note. She had left without a word. But why? Now I remembered telling her that I was straight, and she had said something about me regretting it in the morning. But I had told her that I wouldn't. But she must have thought I said that because of the alcohol. But no, I hadn't. If she had been here, I would have done it with her again—here and now. But then why? Why would a straight girl like me suddenly behave like a lesbian? Was I always a lesbian and I had not known it? To check this out, I thought of a famous and beautiful actress and imagined what I would have done if she had tried to seduce me. I found that thought disgusting. I then thought of another actress, but again I found myself disgusted. Then I thought of this girl, and I found myself getting aroused. Why? She seemed like an exception. Perhaps she invoked in me some kind of long-suppressed fetish. But now she was gone. Maybe if I go to the same bar again tonight, I will see her. And the thought of the bar made me think of Jay. Oh. Oh! I had just messaged him and ran away with that girl. I looked for my phone. It was on the side table. I almost pounced on it. I had to see if Jay had messaged or called. There had been a call from him. But there were too many messages. Oh, how was I going to explain it to him? But I had to first check his messages. I opened the app.

As I went through Jay's messages, my head started spinning all the more. First I was confused as to what the hell he was talking about. Then I saw that he had replied to two of my videos. I had sent him two videos! I clicked on the first video. And then my entire world collapsed around me. This must be a dream, I thought. This must all be a nightmare. It couldn't be true. But it was. That girl, that freak had recorded my videos with her and sent them to Jay. The phone slid out of my hands. I got out of bed and went to the bathroom. Perhaps, I would wake out of this nightmare once my body is clean. Perhaps, a good bath would dissolve all events from the previous night.

I dried my body and came out of the bathroom and checked my phone again. But bad luck sticks to us, doesn't it? We can't wash it away. The videos and the subsequent conversation were still there, glaring at me. That girl had deceived me—I wanted to tell that to Jay. I hadn't known she was a girl. But then in the second video, I had admitted that I didn't care if she was a girl. And what the hell was I thinking about? My explanation didn't mean anything at all. It would only mean I was ready to cheat on my boyfriend with a man. Oh, this hangover and this mess! What had I got myself into? There was no explanation. Jay had already broken up with me on chat. I didn't reply to any of his messages. Not that he wanted a reply. And there was nothing to reply. I kept down the phone and wept for hours.

I dreaded going to the office on Monday. How was I going to face Jay? I would have to avoid him. I felt ashamed. I had not only lost my boyfriend but also the best friend I had. I reached the office and sat at my desk. Lonely. Sad. Ashamed. Feeling cheated by that girl and by destiny. I was hurt and it pained me so much. What had I done to anyone that fate did this to me? And then I remembered Riya. I had laughed at her. I had snatched away her prospective boyfriend from her. And now what would Jay do? Go back to her? Oh no. I lost Jay to that two-plaited weird girl. But would she accept him now? Oh, why not? She would be waiting with her arms open. I hated Riya. And I was again thinking badly about her. What wrong had she ever done to me? Nothing at all. Please forgive me. I was wrong. I was bad. I am bad. Please forgive me, Riya.

CHAPTER TEN

Jay:

I was a fool. And I am not referring to my ditching Riya for Beena. Yes, that too was foolish. But I had no way of knowing what Beena would do. I was a fool when in a weak moment, I went and told my friends that Beena had cheated on me with a girl. At that time, it felt fine. I wanted sympathy from my friends. But instead of evoking sympathy in them, I had become a laughing stock. They would have still accepted Beena cheating on me with a man. But Beena had sex with a girl. Where does that leave me? They just thought Beena was so desperate to satisfy her sexual desires that she had to have sex with anyone who could give her that pleasure. And that meant I couldn't give her what she needed. Those so-called friends made me feel inadequate small, tiny. Was that really the reason that Beena cheated on me? Was it really my fault? If Riya ever came to know about it, would she think she was fortunate that I dumped her? And now instead of grieving about my breakup with Beena, I was worrying about my reputation. I was a fool to have tried to gain sympathy.

CHAPTER ELEVEN

Riya:

Wednesday came and went. I didn't see Priya. Will she ever meet me again? If I had been a homosexual, I would have been her girlfriend. She was a good friend. She cared about me. I cared about her too. But I was a heterosexual. I had hurt her but unintentionally. I couldn't help it.

I had stopped going regularly to sit by the seaside after Priya said she would not meet me for a while. I was going there only on Wednesdays. But it was Friday and I was waiting for her. I wanted to share something with her. If she had come two days back on Wednesday, I wouldn't have had this news that I had today. Oh Priya, where are you? I want to tell you something.

"Hi Riya," Priya said softly as usual from behind me.

I smiled and turning my head to the right, I looked back.

"Sit," I said. "I want to tell you something."

"I thought so," she said. "In fact, I was going to come on Wednesday, but I wanted to give you time."

"What are you talking about?"

"You tell me first what you want to say. Then I will tell you my little secret."

"Hmmm... OK."

"Yes, tell me," she said as she settled down on my right.

"I think something is wrong between Jay and Beena. I see Jay alone nowadays. No, I am not following him. Don't raise your eyebrows like that. After he dumped me, I used to see them together at almost all times. This week, I have not seen them even once together. Maybe they had a fight, but from Jay's body language, I am quite sure they broke up. He doesn't even look in her direction. He behaves as if she does not exist."

"And you keep looking at him to see if he looks at Beena."

"No. I once saw them in the corridor. He was talking to a friend. She passed by. He didn't even look at her. She also walked away with her head down. That's when I started observing them."

"You excited?"

"No. I mean, I was excited to tell you about it. But otherwise, no."

"Why? What if he comes back to you?"

"I will say no."

"Why? Because you have now got me?" said Priya; I think she likes to embarrass me.

"Priya! Don't flirt. It makes me feel guilty. I know I am hurting you, but there is nothing I can do about it. I am really very sorry."

"Now don't say sorry. It makes me feel guilty. But tell me why would you say no to him if he comes back to you."

"I don't know. But till last week I was avoiding him, being self-conscious about my feelings and obsessed about him. But now when I think they have broken up, I don't feel much about anything."

"So you have got your closure."

"Oh. I didn't think about it that way, but now that you say it... I think you are right."

"See I told you I am your right-hand man."

"Huh?" I was confused.

Did she...? Why did she keep saying she was my right-hand man? And didn't she say she was going to meet me on Wednesday but didn't because she wanted to give me time? Time for what? Was she in any way responsible...? And now she was smiling.

"Priya?"

"Yes, Riya?"

"Did you...? How is that even possible? No. No. It may just be my imagination. It's not possible..."

"Now you are talking to yourself."

"Maybe. So now why don't *you* talk to me?"

"You got your closure, Riya. I wanted that. And I tried my best for that."

"How...? But how?" I was stunned.

CHAPTER TWELVE

Priya:

Riya is such an innocent girl. I like that about her. I told her how I had found Beena and Jay on social media.

"So the work you were referring to," Riya said, "was this. That was why you said you might not see me again."

"Yes. How could I meet you if I couldn't find closure for you?"

"And then what did you do?"

And so I told her the details, including how I managed to seduce Beena and send the videos to Jay.

"And even after sending the videos to Jay, you stayed there for the night and you had sex with Beena?!" Riya looked shocked.

"Yes. Why? You jealous?"

"No. Shut up, Priya."

"OK. OK," I said smiling. "But why wouldn't I stay the night at Beena's place? Why not complete what I started? Hadn't I told you that I found Beena sexy? Why not extract pleasure from the task that I was doing? And even Beena received pleasure out of the act. I would have stopped obviously if she had objected to anything. She wanted to continue even after she came to know that I was a woman. I didn't do anything wrong. But yes, I admit that her pleasure was short-lived. She must have cursed herself after knowing that I had sent Jay the videos. I stayed at Beena's place till the morning because it would have been too late to go home at night. But I woke up early and left without telling her. I was sure she would wake up late. She had had a lot to drink. And you can guess what happened after she got up. Can't you? Whatever you observed this week was a result of my doing. And didn't you want this too? Didn't you want your closure?"

"I wanted my closure but this... I don't think I wanted this," Riya said with a serious face.

"Then how did you want your closure?"

"I am not sure."

"Didn't you want revenge?"

"I wanted revenge but on Beena. I didn't want to hurt Jay."

"What? How could you get your revenge on Beena without hurting Jay? And wasn't Jay responsible too?"

"I don't know how I could avenge myself without hurting Jay. Yes, Jay was responsible but he didn't hurt me on purpose. It was unintentional. He cared; he didn't want to hurt me."

"Oh come on. Don't be so naïve. A bit of self-control on his part could have saved you a lot of pain. Stop calling that unintentional. He knew exactly what he was doing when he agreed to go with you on a date. And to kiss you after that..."

"I know. I know. But still, I didn't want to hurt Jay."

"So go to him and tell him that you love him. He will accept you as his girlfriend instantly. He will forget his affair with Beena and be with you."

"But I don't love him anymore."

"You know why you don't love him. That's because you got your closure. And you got your closure because both Jay and Beena were hurt because of their breakup. And still, you say, you didn't want that."

"I wanted that, perhaps. You may be right. But I wouldn't have done what you did. I wouldn't have actually conspired to bring about their breakup."

"And that's why I did it."

"I did not tell you to do it, Priya."

"Oh. So now I am the villain. It's all my fault. You are the hero—a saint."

"No, Priya. I am not blaming you for anything. I know you did it for me. All I am saying is you shouldn't have."

"Well, in the words that you may understand: I did not hurt Jay on purpose; it was *totally unintentional*. I was only hurting Beena."

"You know you are not speaking the truth," Riya said.

She was right because she knew that I knew that unless they both were hurt, she would not have her closure. Riya wanted revenge, but she could not hurt Jay. Especially now that he was already hurt, she felt a soft corner for him.

"I am leaving now," I said in frustration.

"Please don't... OK. If you don't want to stay, it's fine. But meet me tomorrow or maybe later."

"I don't know," I said and started to walk away.

"I will be here on Wednesdays, waiting for you, Priya. Meet me," she pleaded, but I didn't look back.

I know Riya was now feeling bad for me and that was why she wanted to meet me. She is so irritatingly nice. Yes, nice. And maybe she was right. I shouldn't have hurt Jay. Not that I now thought he was not in the wrong, but because somewhere deep down in my heart I knew that hurting Jay would ultimately hurt Riya and I didn't want that. And that made me wrong. Oh, forgive me, Riya, please. She loved Jay, and she didn't want to hurt him. I loved Riya, but I hurt her. That was how I was wrong. I just realised that I loved Riya even now. If I still loved her, that meant helping Riya get closure did not lead me to my closure. So I hurt Riya for nothing. Oh no. Riya, please forgive me. What the hell am I thinking?—I scolded myself. I was the hero. Why then suddenly was I blaming myself? I love you, Riya. I hurt you, Riya. Forgive me, Riya. I went home with confused thoughts. I wanted closure too, but I didn't get one. My love for Riya didn't go away the way her love for Jay disappeared. I was still in a lot of pain. The triumph of hurting Beena and Jay was short-lived. Riya's reaction took it away from me. My hopes for closure: Riya, you took them away. I would get closure now only when I hurt you. No. Nooo... What was I thinking? I could never hurt Riya. Forgive me for thinking that way. Forgive me.

'You need salvation.'

What? Who said that?

'It's me, your saviour.'

But who are you?

'Don't you trust me? Come to me, and I will free you from all your wrong deeds.'

I can save myself.

'If you could, you would have already.'

That's true. But I don't trust anyone.

'Fine then. Be as you are—helpless, confused, hurt and in pain.'

Yes, I am in pain. Will you alleviate it?

'Yes.'

Then do it.

'You will have to come to me for that.'

How should I?

'Change. Change the world.'

Sorry, I don't get you.

Silence. I didn't get a reply. Who just spoke to me, I didn't know. It was like a connection. It was like someone really cared for me. More than even Riya. Riya cared but she had limitations. She couldn't cross the line that divides homosexuals and heterosexuals. This voice did not ask me about my sexual orientation. She—the owner of this voice—wanted to help me unconditionally. But how?

Days passed as if in a dream. I didn't remember much about what happened in those days. It was as if a blur. And that intermittent voice in my head, it was irritating. Then came Wednesday, and I knew Riya would be waiting for me. I had no choice. I didn't want to meet her. But she never left any choice for me. It was as if I could sense her calling me and as if hypnotised, I went to her. Last Wednesday too, when I had decided to give her time so that before she met me she could notice Jay's breakup with Beena, I went to the seaside even when I didn't want to meet her. I went and stared at her. I didn't meet her then. But not so today. Riya was waiting, and I had to meet her.

I stood behind Riya and was about to say hi.

'Don't meet her.'

You again. Why shouldn't I meet her?

'What has she given you? You helped and she rejected your help.'

I love her and I will meet her.

'Don't tell her about me.'

Why not? Are you afraid of her?

'I am afraid of nothing. But she is an obstacle. I will save you. She will push you deep into darkness.'

Whatever.

CHAPTER THIRTEEN

Riya:

"Hi Riya," Priya said, looking haggard, and I felt a pang of sympathy for her.

"I am so glad you came, Priya. Only if you had been a man or I a homosexual, I would have been your girlfriend."

Why did I say that?

"Why would you say that, Riya?"

"Because I care for you. I love you as a friend. But just that. I can't go further."

"Ah, what push? What darkness? Just shut up," Priya said, holding her head.

"What?" I said, feeling offended.

"No Riya. I didn't say that to you."

"Then to whom?"

"This voice in my head. It's irritating. It distracts me, disturbs me."

"What voice?"

"It says things. Since I last met you, it has been there."

"Did you go to a doctor?"

"You mean a psychiatrist? No, Riya. I have not gone mental."

"No, you haven't. But a doctor might help."

"Don't say anything about help. This voice also promises to help."

"Please. I will accompany you."

I felt worried. What was wrong with her? I had never seen her that way.

"No, it's OK. I will talk to her... it, and ask her to stop and leave."

"You talk to the voice?"

"What would you do if you heard a voice?"

"I would go to a doctor."

"I am not going anywhere."

"Would you give me your number? I tried to find you on social media. But..."

"I am not there. And hadn't we agreed that our friendship didn't require all this? It's better this way, isn't it?"

"Yes, but I am worried now."

"Don't worry. If I can get you your closure, I can help myself. Oh, this word 'help' is nauseating."

"Priya, listen to me..."

"I don't want to listen to anyone anymore."

"But I am your friend."

"You have the limitations of being straight. You can't help a lesbian like me."

"I am there for you."

"You cannot be the right-hand-man of your right-hand-man," Priya said and smiled for the first time today, and I felt a bit relieved to see her smile.

"OK. OK. Agreed. But come and meet me daily like the old times."

"No," said Priya emphatically, and I was afraid she might just leave.

"OK. Then every Wednesday? You will meet me here, won't you?"

"Maybe."

"I will wait for you here, Priya."

"Yes. OK. I will try. I have to go now," she said and left.

And I looked at her till she lost herself in a distant crowd. I was worried for her. Voice in her head? That was serious. I read a lot. At least, used to, till Jay came into my life. But what I have read about voices in the head is worrisome. It's a symptom of a psychiatric disorder called schizophrenia. Schizophrenia affects a person mentally. He or she starts living in a different world. And that imaginary world interferes with their day-to-day lives. Was this the start of schizophrenia? That's why I told Priya to visit a doctor. I recognised the symptoms. I had never seen her that way—unkempt hair, haggard look. And perhaps that was the reason I said that I could have been her girlfriend if I had been a homosexual. I just wanted to be there for her. But she didn't seem to be affected much by what I said. I just hope, really hope that voice leaves her alone. I can't bear to see Priya schizophrenic. But if she is, what triggered it in her? Her love for me? My rejection of her? My rejection of her even after she helped me? Am I responsible? Oh no. I am responsible for her condition. Oh, someone, please help me. Please help me help her out of this. Shut up, I told myself. It has just been a week, Priya said, that the voice has been disturbing her. Maybe it's nothing. Maybe she will overcome whatever it is. She may just be depressed. Maybe I am just being paranoid.

After that day, I waited daily for Priya but she didn't come. But on Wednesday, I was hopeful. I waited and waited, time refusing to pass by. But as I saw the sun touch the surface of the sea, I became frustrated and anxious. Oh Priya, please. I just hope you are fine. My mind was totally focussed on my friend. I looked around but didn't see her. I am waiting, Priya. I will wait for you even after sunset today. I closed my eyes, buried my face in my hands and waited. Waited for her soft voice to say 'Hi Riya.'

When my eyes opened, I saw white. White light? No probably, something painted white. A room? My eyes closed again. I don't know how long it was after I opened my eyes again. Again the same white light. I couldn't keep my eyes open and my eyelids dropped close. But then again, I opened my eyes. I was in a hospital room. Everything I saw around was painted white. A dream perhaps, I thought. I was feeling drowsy. A doctor approached me.

"What's your name?" he asked.

"Riya."

"Do you remember how you reached here?"

"No. I was going to ask you the same question. What am I doing here?"

I tried to get up. The doctor stopped me.

"Take it easy."

"Why? What happened to me? What have you done to me?"

"Me? I did nothing. I am a psychiatrist. The other doctors saved your life."

"A psychiatrist? Why?"

"I was always interested in psychology."

"No. I mean, what are you doing here with me? And first of all, what happened to me?"

"We will take it up slowly. Session by session."

"What?"

"Take rest now. We will meet in the morning in my office."

The next day, I found myself sitting in front of the doctor. I looked at my left hand. It was bandaged at the wrist.

"Will anyone tell me what's going on?" I demanded. "Or else I will have to call the police."

"The police are already here. But we prefer you talk to me first rather than them. Even you would like to talk to me first."

I looked at the psychiatrist with wide eyes.

"Do you really not remember how you ended up here?"

"No. And what happened to my wrist?" I demanded again.

"It's slit."

"What?"

"It's slit."

"I heard you the first time."

"Then why did you ask?" asked the doctor matter-of-factly.

I was now exasperated. I decided not to say anything. And it worked, kind of. He started speaking.

"Someone found you near the seaside? You were unconscious because of the loss of a lot of blood. You were brought here, and the doctors saved your life. Do you still want to talk to the police first?"

"So I surmise you are assuming that I cut my wrist and tried to commit suicide. And since suicide is a crime, you think I wouldn't call the police?"

"Smart," he commented.

"But the police won't be able to do anything. They would have let me off even if I had actually tried to commit suicide. Those cases are sensitive, and the police never get involved. They let the doctors take the entire responsibility of the person."

"See, you tell me why you did it, and we can find some way to prevent you from being sent to jail."

"Really?" I said and laughed.

"The police are pressuring us. They want this case closed. I have been assigned the task of finding out why you did it. Tell us, and after a few sessions of psychotherapy, we will let you go."

"But why would I accept trying to commit suicide when I know it's not the truth?"

"So what do you think about slit wrist? Who must have done that to you?"

This question jolted me out of my non-cooperation with the doctor. Who could have done that to me? I thought I knew the answer. It had to be Priya. A disgruntled homosexual lover. But I didn't want to take her name. I didn't want to implicate her. I suspected her to be suffering from schizophrenia, but if I mentioned her, the police would overlook and ignore her condition purposely in a hurry to close the case. Priya was a friend. I couldn't see her behind the bars.

"What are you thinking?"

"Nothing."

"I think you know who did this to you."

"No, I don't know. I just know I didn't try to commit suicide."

"You will be prolonging the closure of the case if you are uncooperative. The police will still assume you tried to do it. This means they will want us to keep you under observation while they find the person and charge him with attempted murder. And you may have to stay here in the psychiatric ward for a long time."

"What? You are lying."

"OK. Try it."

I was sure the psychiatrist was using psychology against me. But what if he was telling the truth? My job—what would happen of it? My parents—what would happen to them when they learn their daughter is in a mental asylum? Should I mention Priya and get done with it or should I accept that I tried committing suicide? But if I admit to trying to commit suicide, they will still keep me here.

"I have no reason to commit suicide," I said just to buy time.

"Then have you given a reason to anyone to murder you?"

"No. But can't it be some mentally disturbed stranger?"

"See, they tested you for molestation or rape. They found no evidence. Except for your slit wrist, there was nothing on your body to suggest that someone else did it to you. Why try to kill someone without a motive?"

"Then why would I try to kill myself without a motive? Moreover, I said a mentally disturbed person may have tried to kill me. Do such people require motives?"

"OK. Tell me something about yourself," the doctor said, ignoring my argument, and I became sure he was trying to prove that I had done it.

Instead of continuing the argument and making him feel I was not cooperative, I told him about my life in the village. I told him how I had come here to the city in search of a job.

"How did you adjust to the city, given your simple life in the village?"

Wow, I thought. If I told him about how I was teased at my office about my two plaits, he would certainly feel I was depressed and then try to prove I had a reason for suicide.

"Will you stop thinking," he said, "and answer my questions? If you take so much time answering my questions, I will have to assume you are lying."

I gulped and he saw that.

"Come on now," he said. "We are here to help. Trust me I will believe you if your story sounds credible."

I looked into his eyes. He seemed to be a fine person after all. But he was a psychiatrist. He was just using psychology to make me talk. But did I have an option?

"It was difficult to adjust to the city in the beginning. New people, you know. But I adjusted to it after a while. No big deal."

"Tell me about your life in the past few months."

"Nothing much. Just the routine. Job, home. That's all."

"What were you doing there at the seaside?"

"Watching the sea and the sunset. I do it often."

"All by yourself? No friend?"

Shit, I thought. He is asking all the difficult questions.

"I am a loner. Always was."

"So you have few friends. Who are your friends here in the city?"

I just looked at him. With every question, it was becoming all the more difficult to convince him that I didn't do it.

"No one?" he asked.

"I have friendly colleagues," I lied.

"So only colleagues. No friends."

"No real friends," I had to admit.

"How do you cope with that?"

"I don't have to cope up. As I said, I am a loner. It doesn't affect me. I am in fact glad that I didn't make any real friends here. That way I don't need to conform to societal expectations and pressure."

"So there are societal pressures," he said, scribbling something on his notepad.

"Yes. But nothing serious because I don't mind being alone and I don't care."

"Who is your closest colleague at your office?"

I wanted to wriggle out of this interrogation, but I was unable to find a way.

"No one in particular. I go there to do my job, not make friends."

"Were you friends with anyone when you were at your native place?"

"Yes but not a close friendship with anyone."

"OK. Tell me the names of your childhood friends."

I told him three names.

"And here in the city, you have none," he noted.

"Correct."

"Any lover? A crush at your office?"

"None."

"Who were you waiting for at the seaside yesterday?" he asked, and I looked at him with surprised and guilty eyes.

How did he know I was waiting for someone? And then I realised my mistake. I instantly averted his gaze, but he had seen my expression. So foolish of me, I thought. He had repeated the question but paraphrased it. He was bombarding me with questions and in my haste to reply, which I thought would convince him I wasn't lying, I missed the fact that he had already asked me this question in a different way, which I had already answered.

"So, you were indeed waiting for someone," he smiled.

"I want my lawyer," I said.

"I am not the police and this is not an interrogation," he said and chuckled. "Stop playing games now, Riya. Tell me the truth."

"How do I know you are not helping the police close the case the way they want it?"

"You don't. And you can never know. You will have to trust me or not trust me. But I would prefer that you do and tell me the truth."

My face fell. I was defeated.

"I will speak the truth but I have a request. I think I know who did this to me. But I am not sure. Moreover, the person who, I think, did this to me might be suffering from a mental illness. If you ignore that and let that person be arrested, it will not be justice."

"OK. I will listen to what you have to say. And if I am convinced about what you have just told me, I will try to help. Trust me on this."

And so I started at the beginning because if I had to tell anyone about Priya, the background was necessary.

Office. The ridiculing of the two-plaited girl. Jay. My crush. His rejection of me. Beena. And finally, my saviour, Priya. Her helping me out. Her being a homosexual. Her falling in love with me. Her revenge on Beena on my behalf. I getting my closure but losing Priya as a friend. The voice in her head. My suspicion that she was schizophrenic. My waiting yesterday. But her absence and my landing up at the hospital with a slit wrist.

"That's all," I said. "Maybe she was schizophrenic before she met me and I didn't know about it. But she never mentioned the voice in her head until a few days back. Maybe my rejection of her triggered something in her brain. She believed that she would get her closure when I got mine. I got mine because of her, but I didn't approve of the way she did it because that hurt Jay too along with Beena. My disapproval of Priya's means of revenge kind of estranged her from me. And she didn't get her closure which might have been my appreciation of her which I denied her because of our difference in opinion. I don't really know who slit my wrist and how it was done. I last remember waiting for Priya at the seaside. But if Priya is the one who did it, please help her. I had told her I would accompany her to a psychiatrist, but look at the irony of the situation. I am the one who is in front of you, trying to deny that I am depressed. I am not depressed anymore. I had got my closure. So do you now, believe me, doctor? I did not try to commit suicide."

The doctor remained silent for a long time. He kept looking at me. But it was a blank stare. It seemed he was lost in thought. Then he breathed in deeply and sighed.

"Call her," the doctor said.

"Who? Priya?"

"Who else?"

"But I don't have her phone number. She is not on any social networking site either."

"Just as I thought."

"Meaning?"

"She was or is your best friend. In fact, the only one in the city, and you don't have her phone number. And if my suspicion is correct, you don't even know where she lives."

"Yes. I don't know that too. We never..."

"Why?"

"We thought that was a better way. Our friendship didn't need..."

"Excuses."

"No, doctor. Please believe me. I am not trying to protect her by lying to you."

"I believe you. The thing is I don't trust what you believe."

I was confused. I was unable to understand what he was getting at.

"Tell me how she looks," the doctor said.

"You need the description to help the police find her?"

"No. I want you to describe her. I am not a sketch artist. I am a psychiatrist."

"OK," I said, still confused. "She has short hair like a boy's."

"Her height?"

"She is this tall," I said, lifting my right hand above my head."

"Stand up and tell me."

I stood up, looked at my side, imagined Priya there and lifted my hand."

"So she is as tall or short as you," concluded the doctor.

"Yes, I guess," I said.

"And her eyes? Let me guess. Large eyes. And lips? Full lips. Eyebrows not too thin or too thick. Slightly sharp nose. Ear lobes attached. You know what attached ear lobes are, don't you? The majority of people have free ear lobes because the gene that causes the attached ear lobes is a recessive gene. Recessive means the gene which is not dominant. A person has to have two recessive genes to cause that trait to manifest. One gene to be received from the father and one from the mother. Both genes should be recessive, otherwise, the earlobes that form will be of the dominant trait, that is, free ear lobes."

"Yes, I am aware of the attached ear lobes and the recessive genes. But how do you know so much about Priya's looks? Did she come to you for her condition?"

The doctor smiled. It was a knowing smile. I didn't understand.

"Go and stand in front of the mirror, Riya."

I did as commanded.

"Observe yourself," said the doctor. "What do you see? Large eyes, sharp nose. Shapely eyebrows. Full lips. You are beautiful, Riya. And so is Priya. And do you see your ear lobes? How are they? Attached, right?"

I looked at my reflection and back at the doctor with bewildered eyes.

"Come back and take your seat," he said and I obeyed.

"It's just a coincidence..."

The doctor almost laughed.

"Do you still think it's a coincidence that your only friend in this city looks like you?"

"She has short hair, and I have long hair."

"Yeah. Yeah. I know. You said that. And you also told me that you were laughed at because of your long hair which you styled in two plaits."

"So?" I demanded.

"So Priya looks everything like you except for the hair. No plaits. No ridicule."

"What are you getting at, doctor?" I asked, now irritated.

"You know it, Riya. You wanted to save yourself from the depression you were under after Jay broke up with you. You didn't have a friend. So you created one. It was all well-planned. No, I am not saying you planned it consciously. But your subconscious planned it quite well. You are a logical person. So your brain decided to create a friend who is not on any social media. You decided not to exchange phone numbers. How can you when the other person does not exist? Or rather, I should say, you two are the same person. Riya is Priya. Priya is Riya. Riya with a P. Your brain created a friend who you yourself would not decipher as imaginary. Great. You are intelligent, Riya. Even in your condition, your intelligence is apparent."

"What you say makes no sense," I said bluntly. "And what condition are you talking about?"

"Multiple personality disorder. You ever heard about that?"

"Yes, I know about it. And I also know now that you are just a pawn in the hands of the police."

The doctor smiled sadly. And seeing him sad made me feel bad about what I said to him. Maybe he was trying his best, but he had got it all wrong. What rubbish! But I should say he was intelligent. To have concocted such a story needs intelligence. But still, he was wrong.

"OK. What about Priya's sexual orientation?" I asked just to find out what the doctor would say about that.

"Priya, a girl, a woman, would fall in love with you only if she was a lesbian. And falling in love with you would flatter your ego. At least there was someone who could love you. Heterosexuality or homosexuality didn't matter. What mattered was you feeling loved. You got that from Priya."

"Enough. Enough. You cannot convince me that Priya doesn't exist."

"Yes. Enough for today. Your brain won't be able to take more of it. Slowly, gradually, you will be able to accept the facts though. You are intelligent, and I am sure you will see the truth one day. If you don't, you will not see the outside world."

"You are threatening me. That if I don't see it your way, you will not let me go."

"No, it's not a threat. I am just trying to help you. Help yourself and be free."

"I will leave now." Saying that, I got up.

"One last question," he said.

I looked at him but remained silent.

"Why is it that you never saw Priya approach you? Why did she always *talk* first and then appear? Isn't that what happened? Think about it. And she did come and meet you when you yearned for her presence. Even when you didn't expect her to come, she just came. Am I right?"

I didn't reply.

Doctor:

Riya had long gone. But I remained seated in my chair. She had a long way to go. So many questions! And she needed the answers to those. Only logical answers would convince her. And the mind has all the answers. It's written in our scriptures. For every question in the universe or even about the universe, the mind has an answer to each of them. Because we are one with the universe. We are the universe.

I slowly got up from my seat. Sometimes, my short stature made my feet pain since they did not touch the floor when seated; all chairs were made for taller people. I sighed, stood up and approached the mirror on the wall where Riya had been standing a few minutes back. I looked at my face. Large eyes, sharp nose, shapely eyebrows, full lips. I moved my fingers through my abundant hair and looked at my ears. Attached ear lobes. I was Riya's saviour—a personality who could pull her out of her imaginary world. And if I was Riya's saviour, then how different could I look from her? I was just a reflection of her mind—the mind out to find the truth. The reflection in the mirror changed from me to Priya to Riya. Then the mirror dissolved and vanished. All I saw now was a white wall of the hospital.

CHAPTER FIFTEEN

Riya:

I opened my eyes. I was on the hospital bed. My hands were tied to the bed. I had to lift my head strenuously to check. My left hand was bandaged at the wrist. I saw a nurse.

"How much time have I been here?" I asked her.

"Since yesterday evening."

"Was I unconscious?"

"Yes, for the first part. Then we sedated you."

"What? Why? But forget that. Did I talk to a doctor?"

"How could you when you were sedated?"

"Why is my left wrist bandaged?"

"As if you don't know... I will call the doctor," saying that, the nurse went out.

So the psychiatrist was a dream. Well, perhaps not a dream, but something like that. At least not real. But how did he or I know about my slit wrist when I had just woken up and had no memory of any incident involving the attempted suicide or murder? Perhaps my brain sensed the pain in my hands and made up a story. Perhaps the psychiatrist was actually a dream! No. No. It couldn't be. The logic that was involved... Was I really suffering from multiple personality disorder? Did Priya not exist? But if Priya did not exist, who slit my hand? Was it me? Those thoughts were tiring because all this was confusing. I closed my eyes, but someone called my name.

"Hi. I am your doctor."

I opened my eyes to find a policeman accompanying a doctor. The usual procedure, I thought.

"What happened?" I asked.

"You don't remember?" asked the policeman.

"No," I replied.

"Retrograde amnesia," mumbled the doctor.

"Huh?" the policeman looked at the doctor for some explanation.

"We will talk outside." The doctor said.

"No need," I interrupted. "I know what retrograde amnesia is. It means there was some traumatic incident involving me, and my brain has forgotten the incident along with a few minutes before it. It may be psychological. The doctor thinks I have retrograde amnesia. It may be because my brain would like to forget what happened to avoid further stress. Well, what I remember is being at the seaside. Then nothing. Please tell me what happened."

"That's why we have come here, to find out what happened to you," said the policeman.

"Meaning?" I asked.

"Your left wrist was slit. Blood was flowing like water. A passer-by saw you and called the ambulance and the police."

"And you all think I tried to commit suicide?"

"Well...," said the doctor.

"It's OK. You can tell me. But believe me, I am not depressed. I have no intention of killing myself."

"We will talk later," said the policeman. "I have recorded your statement for now. Are you right-handed..."

"Did anyone actually see what happened?" I asked, interrupting him.

"No. It was after sunset and quite dark, and the person who saw you did not see anyone else around you," replied the policeman. "Are you right-handed? Can you sign? I will write your name and address. Then read your statement and sign."

"Yes."

"Tell me your name and address," the policeman said.

"Riya," I told him my name. But don't you know my name? I mean did anyone find my purse?"

"There was nothing with you when we found you."

"Someone stole my purse even when I was bleeding? Or did someone do it for my purse? My phone..."

"Does your phone have a pin to unlock?"

"Yes," I replied.

"Then don't worry. There is not much that can be done with your phone. But to be on the safer side, get your SIM and other cards deactivated?"

"I am in a hospital. Who's paying the bill?"

"It's a government hospital. Don't worry about it for now," this time the doctor replied.

I looked around. This didn't look like a government hospital.

"I know," said the doctor and smiled. "This doesn't look like a government hospital. We recently received a donation. Some part of this institution was renovated."

He then released my right hand. The policeman asked for a few details and asked me to sign. I did. The duo then left. I lay there silently. I had so many questions, but no one whom I could ask. After a while, I drifted back to sleep.

It might have been a few hours later that I woke up.

"Can someone free my hands?" I said; someone had tied my right hand again.

A nurse walked in.

"We don't have the permission to do that."

"Did anyone call my family?"

"We didn't. Maybe the police did after you gave them your details. You didn't have any ID on you."

"Yes. OK," I said.

I didn't think the police would have called. They do everything at the last minute when it becomes an absolute necessity. And I was not dead; so there was no hurry. I had no issue though. Why call my parents and make them worry? I can do it when I am out of here, I thought. Since this was a police case, and I was suspected of an attempted suicide, it might take some time but I hoped they would discharge me soon.

I had expected that I would be consulted by a psychiatrist. But when they would take me to him or her, that I didn't know. But the wait wasn't long. I wasn't in a critical state. So they could take me to the psychology department. Well, on a wheelchair. I told them I could walk as my ankles and feet were fine and only one of my wrists was slit, but they insisted. I gave up. When I reached the small room where the psychiatrist was waiting, the ward boy asked me to stand up and shift to a chair opposite the doctor's. I asked him if he was sure I should get up or if he was going to lift me and place me there. The ward boy seemed annoyed with my question, but the doctor chuckled. I shifted to the comfortable chair. The ward boy took the wheelchair away.

"Hey, I will need it to get back," I said.

The ward boy looked at me and tried again to show his annoyance but couldn't suppress his smile.

I looked at the doctor. I was already irritated. And now I would have to face the same questions again. I had already had a session with a doctor in my dream and now this one. But this time, apart from the irritating questions, there was one more problem. For the last few hours, I had been thinking. I had started believing what the doctor in my dream told me. I wasn't entirely sure but that imaginary doctor's diagnosis had some logic in it. Why was Priya's name Priya? Why did it contain my name, Riya? The more I thought I realised the dream-doctor was right in making me realise that Priya looked almost like me. Now that I thought about it, the dream-doctor himself looked like me. And moreover, it was plausible but still highly improbable that Priya was not on any of the social media. I too am a loner, but still, I use social media to be in touch with my family and some of my friends from my village. Sometimes even for some office work. And wasn't it convenient (or inconveniently impractical) not to share our phone numbers with each other? My brain didn't require the complication of our sharing the same number with each other. It had found a bypass around the problem. My brain did not want me to realise that Priya and Riya were the same. Then why now? Perhaps because I had got my closure now, my brain was showing me reality. But then what kind of closure was that if nothing really happened? Yet, I felt free, that is, I was no longer in love with Jay. So maybe it was indeed closure, and so my brain had started crumbling the imaginary world I was living in. But I didn't know the answers to all the questions I had. Sometimes Priya being only in my imagination seemed impossible. She had to be real, I thought. And if Priya didn't exist and she didn't slit my wrist, then who did? But still, I was now open to the possibility that I might be suffering from multiple personality disorder. If that was true, I must have had hallucinations. And I didn't know which experience was real and which I had imagined. Now, sitting in front of this doctor, I wondered if this was real or my imagination. And I could tell the psychiatrist that I had diagnosed myself and that I was suffering from multiple personality disorder. But then which mental patient had gone to a psychiatrist and told it on his face that he had made the diagnosis, that he was mad and that he needed help? It would seem absurd. Moreover, if I were to tell this doctor my diagnosis of myself, he would assume that I was lying to protect myself from the police. And this was the other problem in addition to the boring questions I was about to face. So I kept my problem aside. I would stick to my story that I didn't know anything. I had thought about telling the doctor about Priya and letting him find out that she was my imagination but what if she really existed? I was still not sure about that. It was better to forget the dream-doctor's diagnosis and stick to what I knew or felt was real. I didn't know who slit my wrist, and I would say that. I looked at the doctor with an expression that suggested I was facing an opponent in a duel. And as I looked I realised he looked nothing like me. He seemed much taller and the most important thing was that his ear lobes were free. I sighed. So most probably, I was not in a dream and this psychiatrist in front of me was not a personality that I made up. Or the other possibility was that he was my imaginary saviour but a lesser character in my world of imagination. It becomes so difficult when you can't trust your own brain, when you know what you are seeing might just be a figment of your imagination.

"You know why you are here?" he asked.

"To convince you that I didn't try to commit suicide?" I asked.

"How can you be sure of that when your statement to the police says that you remember being at the seaside but nothing after that?"

"That's because I know I have no reason to kill myself."

"How do I trust you? You may be lying."

"Do I need to prove myself? Or do you need to prove that I have a reason?" I challenged him.

"We don't need to prove anything. Our report will be the final word. After that, it will be very difficult for you to prove us wrong."

"Even if you say that I am suicidal, does it have any practical implications? The court never imposes any real punishment. So what does it matter?" I didn't like his approach, and I felt compelled to argue.

"Your job. Your personal life. You will lose your job. No other company will hire you when they do their background verification. Your personal life will be affected when you try to explain why you don't have a job. What then?"

"So you will spoil my career and my life just to win this argument."

"I will but not to win this argument. I will do it because your slit wrist tells a story. A story which only you can prove wrong. So convince me. At least try. And I don't believe that you don't remember anything. Because I don't think retrograde amnesia will set in in case of an attempted suicide. So don't lie. Just tell me the truth."

"So if I accept that I did it, I will be tagged as suicidal. And even if I fail to convince you, even then I will be suicidal. The end result is the same. So why should I even try to convince you?"

"Because if you didn't do it, then why will we tag you as having suicidal tendencies?"

"And how do I prove it?"

This discussion was going on in circles and I didn't like it. That dream-doctor was better, I thought.

"Let's begin by you telling me what you were doing at the seaside," the psychiatrist said.

"Why? Can't a person enjoy the sunset or the sea breeze?"

"All by herself? Solitude or should I say, loneliness?"

"So you have decided it's loneliness?" I said, now totally irritated.

"You are not cooperative. We need information which only you can provide. But if you are not cooperating then I will have to write my report," saying this the doctor stood up.

I became agitated. He was going to ruin my career for no fault of mine. He was going to ruin my personal life for his ego because he couldn't win an argument with me. But why was I arguing? I should stay calm and cooperate. But I didn't want to because I didn't want to be diagnosed with multiple personality disorder. That too would ruin my life. The doctor was almost at the door now, and my eyes welled up, and tears started rolling down my cheeks. I wanted to stop him, but my ego wouldn't let me do it. I was enraged by his behaviour. I was extremely angry. I lifted my right hand and was going to bang my fist on the table in front of me. But I didn't. Or did I?

CHAPTER SIXTEEN

The Psychiatrist:

I was almost at the door. Well, I wasn't going to storm away dramatically. I was just making Riya feel so. I wanted her to talk. I wasn't going to ruin her life, only making her feel so. Because I wanted to know the truth. Diagnosis lies in truth. We doctors can never be sure if our patient is telling us the truth. We sometimes have to get the information we need by using different methods. Different people react to different stimuli. I found a threat to her career and personal life would work in Riya's case. I should say she is intelligent. Her arguments are intelligent. But the fact is we need the truth for proper diagnosis. Only then we can help our patients. Whether the diagnosis ruins their career or not, that's secondary. We can't lie about a diagnosis. So to help me find the truth, I acted as if I was leaving the room. And it worked. Riya banged her fist on the table. And I stopped and turned around.

"You cannot talk to Riya like that," Riya said, and I should say I was a little taken aback.

I had expected Riya to agree to be cooperative, stop me, and even perhaps plead. But I had not expected this.

"You cannot speak to Riya like that," she repeated, and I realised only now that she was referring to herself in the third person.

"And who are you to tell me that?" I asked, maintaining the aggression.

"I am Priya, her best friend. Talk to me. I will tell you what you want to know. Riya is soft-hearted. Leave her alone if you want the information you like to seek," Riya said in a voice that was slightly different than before.

She then lifted her plait off her back, wrapped it around her head twice and tucked the free end inside her locks at the back of her head. Priya had a different hairstyle, I could see. I went back to my chair and sat down. I had a story to listen to. The recording was now on.

CHAPTER SEVENTEEN

Priya:

I learned from Riya that her psychiatrist was harassing her. So I accompanied her to a session and took on myself to talk to him. I saw my bandaged left wrist. I knew he would ask me about that. So I moved my left hand quickly from the table to my lap. I wouldn't have been alive here, trying to protect Riya, had I not been saved by my neighbour. He saw a pool of blood coming out of my apartment, and he called the ambulance and the doctors saved me. Perhaps I was meant to live for my love, to protect her.

CHAPTER EIGHTEEN

The Psychiatrist:

The information I got from Priya was valuable though her story had a lot of holes in it. She couldn't logically answer how she came here. She compensated that with her aggression and her need to protect Riya from a harassing doctor who was me. Riya, I now knew, had multiple personality disorder. Priya is, what we call, an alter. A different personality in the same person is called an alter. An alter may or may not be aware of the actual person, but in Riya's case, the alter—Priya—is aware of the actual person—Riya. Alters are different personalities which manifest themselves in the patient when the person perceives an event in their life as a threat. Priya 'arrived' in my conversation with Riya because Riya perceived me as a threat. After a while, I changed my stance and talked politely with Priya. The threat disappeared. Priya perceived me as docile and Riya returned. She looked confused. But she most probably remembered her last argument with me and my patient now became silent.

"Riya?" I said tentatively, not knowing for sure if Riya had actually returned.

But she looked up at me and I became sure.

"Riya, can you tell me who Priya is?"

Riya was surprised, but then she sighed and her shoulders dropped.

"I need a mirror, doctor," she said, surprising me with this weird request.

I looked for one in my drawer and found a small one. I handed it over to her across the table. She looked at herself—her hair. And then she unwound her plait from her head.

"So Priya talked to you?" she said in a defeated voice, handing me back the mirror.

I was stunned. I can't say I had a very long career, but in whatever years of experience I had, I hadn't seen a patient who realised what she was going through.

"Have you been previously diagnosed...?"

"No," Riya replied, "but I have an inkling about what I have."

That's why she asked for the mirror. She wanted to know if Priya had been here.

"How do I know," she asked, "that this conversation here between you and me is real and not my imagination?"

"Right now, I don't have a method to prove it to you, but if I find one, I will use it to convince you."

"Then you must be real," she said, "since you don't have an answer to everything. So where should I start my story?"

I had no idea. I was actually stunned. She was smart, I could say.

"Where do you think you should start?" I asked her.

"I am no longer sure."

"Start at a time where you think you are sure. A remote past maybe. Then we will find out if we need to go back further. But before that, take a look at this."

I did something I had never expected myself to do. I showed her the video where her alter, Priya, was talking to me. I had never done that, not in the first session ever. But Riya was different. She needed to know. I wanted her to know.

Riya was stunned and amazed at how she had transformed into Priya. I was sure she was feeling mentally tired. So I ended the session there. I called the ward boy with the wheelchair to take her back and meanwhile, we waited not doing or saying much. It was then that I noticed her arms. The left forearm was devoid of hair. When did they start shaving hair off of the arms just to sew the slit wrists?—that was my first thought. But of course, that wasn't the case. Riya's waxed left arm versus her right arm with her natural vellus hair might be related to her condition. I would wait till later to judge. Right now, I didn't want to make a remark on it.

I kept my diagnosis pending. But I decided to start with another session the following morning. The protocol remained. She was brought to my office in a wheelchair. Riya didn't protest this time.

"Yes please," I said. "Start with your story."

She started her narration from the time when she came to this city from her native place. And I assumed that she was sure whatever happened before that was not related to the current incidents involving her multiple personalities. I trusted her judgement. I listened. The first incident that might have triggered the need for a protective personality like Priya to be created in her mind seemed to be her bullying at the office because she styled her hair in two plaits. But Priya hadn't been born yet. It was only later after Riya became depressed that an alter was born. This alter later fell in love with Riya. A lesbian lover. Interesting—I thought, given that Riya was straight. But that can happen in patients with Dissociated Identity Disorder. Many such interesting events happen in the lives of these patients. Well, interesting for us doctors, not for the unfortunate people who suffer from the condition. Multiple Personality Disorder is an old term, but we tend to use that for the benefit of the patients. Anyway, Riya herself remained straight even in the company of Priya. She rejected Priya's love. Priya took revenge on Beena and Jay on behalf of Riya. But Riya did not approve of her alter's methods because that hurt Jay who perhaps she still loved. Priya could not take her disapproval. And a few days later, Riya landed up in the hospital. She also mentioned that she thought Priya was suffering from schizophrenia—an interesting diagnosis of her own alter, I thought. But Riya said that her diagnosis no longer mattered now that she realised that Priya only existed in her mind. Riya then mentioned that in her sedated state the night she was brought here, she already had a session with a doctor in her dream. That made her suspect that Priya may actually be her imagination. Riya was irritated when she met me, not knowing what to believe and what not to. And what to tell me. But fortunately or unfortunately, Priya again revealed herself, and that gave me an idea about what her problem was. That was the end of her story. I pulled out yesterday's recording and watched it again. In the recording, I observed how Priya subtly pulled her left hand in her lap away from my view. She did not want me to know that her wrist had been slit. Also, whenever she referred to Riya, Priya subconsciously pointed or gestured towards her left as if Riya was actually sitting there beside her. Hallucinations!—I knew.

"Doctor, I have told you my entire story," Riya said. "But I have a lot of questions. Some parts of my story still make me think Priya actually exists."

"Ah well. Priya is your alter, not a real person. But there is a possibility that Priya's personality that your mind built is based on an actual person you might have met or known in your life. But the Priya you change into does not exist. Let me parse the details of your story for you," I said, shifting the notes that I had taken while Riya was narrating her story.

I looked at my notes.

"First of all," I began, "I should say you are very intelligent. Your brain at a very basic level planned all this. Planned all the details. Almost perfectly. So perfectly that you as Riya wouldn't know that this was all imaginary, and yet you found it out. That, I would say, is amazing. You found out because you got your closure, and you no longer required Priya to intervene in your life or make decisions on your behalf. Your brain now has set itself on the path to healing itself. I cannot guarantee, but this looks promising. An alter is a means to escape from reality. Priya helped you deal with the reality of Jay's rejection of you. Now that you are over it, your brain diagnosed its own condition. This realisation itself is the first step to cure. Again, I will say that cure cannot be guaranteed, but I am hopeful about it."

I looked at my notes again. Priya was imaginary, but she had her own set of memories, which Riya, sitting in front of me wouldn't know. She would only know what Priya told her. Both Riya and Priya's memories, whether they were real or imagined, were present in the person sitting in front of me, and this person's brain might subconsciously be using those sets of memories and mixing them. However, at the conscious level, some of Priya's memories might not be accessible if I talked to Riya and vice versa. Actually, I could prescribe her medication and ask Riya to visit me for follow-ups. But that would not be sufficient. As she said, she had questions, answers to which if she got, could help with her condition. Hypnosis was a method through which I could summon Priya or Riya's subconscious and get some answers. And I told her that. She agreed since she was looking forward to some answers.

It was Priya this time who I had called through hypnosis. I was recording the session as usual. I asked Priya the details of how she seduced Beena. Riya in the form of Priya felt excited as she narrated the story. When she reached the part where she had sex with Beena, I noticed her expression change subtly. I could see her breathing become deeper as if she was reliving the moments. Priya was a lesbian as Riya had mentioned. She mentioned how initially she had felt self-conscious about her unwaxed body hair, but Beena had not minded that at all and perhaps even enjoyed her being natural. Priya, on the other hand, had been turned on by Beena's smooth hairless body. And now I understood why Riya's left arm was hairless while her right arm remained unwaxed. The right half acted as Priya and the left one was supposed to be Beena. And then it struck me like lightning. My eyes widened. I stood up from my chair. Was my suspicion logical? It meant Riya's case might be more complicated than I had thought. The Priya in Riya loved her natural body. She didn't care about the vellus hair on her forearms. If so, why would Priya wax her left forearm? Now there was a possibility that it was not Priya but Riya who did it. But Riya and Priya were almost the same except for the long and short hair. If Priya didn't care about her body hair, it was basically a characteristic of Riya which Priya inherited as her alter. But Beena was supposed to be the villain here. Her likes and dislikes had to be different from Riya's or Priya's. Now if Riya or Priya did not wax their left arm, who did it? It was of course, Beena. And that meant only one thing. And that was Beena too was an alter residing in Riya's brain. It didn't mean that Beena didn't exist in reality. She might or she might not. But she did exist as Riya's alter. I became almost certain of that. I woke Riya up from her trance.

Riya looked at me. First, a confused look till she remembered I had put her under a hypnotic trance. Then an impatient curiosity to know what happened.

"Did we find our answers?" she asked.

"Perhaps more questions," I said thoughtfully.

Should I share my discovery with her? Would she be able to digest it? But wasn't this exercise meant to find answers and help Riya? I decided to tell her. I showed her the video. Then I told her to look at her forearms.

"Why did you wax your left forearm but not the right one?"

Riya became a bit embarrassed about my mention of her body hair. But she replied.

"I may have noticed it before but I did not think about it. But I don't remember having waxed it."

Then I told her about my theory. Beena was an alter, I declared.

"But Beena exists. Or does she not? No, she exists. Will I ever be cured?" she looked anxious.

"I did not say Beena does not exist in reality. But she also exists as your alter. And yes, I am hopeful that you will be cured. But we have to peel off the layers one by one. We are still in the first stages. The more information we have, the more it can be used for your counselling and medication. And if you are open to new discoveries like you are right now, then yes, I feel you can be cured."

I said that more to encourage her, rather than believing it. But that didn't mean I didn't believe she could be cured.

"Why is Priya a homosexual?" Riya asked. "And why and how could my own alter fall in love with myself? Maybe I know the answer to the second question but I want it from you."

"What your dream-doctor told you is correct. After Jay ditched you, you might have started having doubts about yourself. Like maybe no one could ever love you. Priya fell in love with you to give you the confidence that you are indeed a lovable person. Priya is your creation. She is a protagonist in your story. She is very similar to your actual self. Except that she does what you can't. She fights for you and protects you where you fail. This is what you love about Priya, and to be loved by this person gives you confidence. As I said, your brain made this up with quite a lot of planning. Though not for your condition, you should be proud of your intelligence. Your first question: why is Priya a lesbian? A part of the answer lies in the answer to the second question. Priya was supposed to fall in love with you to flatter your ego. You made Priya up as a reflection of yourself. So she had to be a girl or a woman. And since she is a girl, she had to be a lesbian to fall in love with you."

"But I am a heterosexual. How do I turn homosexual and then back?"

"What do you think sexual orientation is? If you ask me, I will say it's just a mindset. Have you heard of heterosexual people who turn homosexual later in life and vice versa? Maybe hormones also play a role. But it's not always that. Sometimes these people think they were always homosexual deep down but due to societal pressures, they suppressed their sexual orientation. But it's not always that either. As I said, it may just be a mindset. Like say you have liked mangoes all your life, but after a certain age, you start liking apples more. Then you start eating this fruit more. And then after a couple of years, you realise that no, mangoes had always been better. Sexual orientation may change. In normal people, it may take years. In people like you with different personalities, it may change in minutes. Do you know a hen can change to a rooster?

Well not genetically, but it can develop the characteristics of a male. In some frogs, sex change happens spontaneously. There was research that said that if the population of elephants increases, the percentage of homosexuality in this species also increases. Sexual orientation might be nature's way of controlling the population. And some of the individuals in a species might be predisposed to this change that nature imposes on them. The spontaneous sex change in lower animals cannot be replicated in higher animals like elephants or humans. That may be the reason why our sexual orientation changes—perhaps this need to change our sexual orientation is a remnant of spontaneous sex change in lower animals. So yes, it should not be surprising that Priya is a lesbian even when you are not. By the way, you may have already guessed it—the doctor or the psychiatrist in your dream was also an alter. So you have three alters—Priya, the doctor and Beena."

"How many more?" Riya asked, looking tired.

I just smiled. I didn't know what to expect after Beena's discovery.

"You know," I said, "your mind gave Priya schizophrenia. Had you not known about the condition called schizophrenia and its symptoms, Priya may not have been schizophrenic."

"Meaning?"

"Once Priya settled the scores with Beena and Jay, you felt avenged. You got your closure. Your mind wanted the scores to be settled that way even if it meant hurting Jay. But a part of you still loved Jay and you disapproved of your own style of revenge. So the part of you who hurt Jay had to go. It had to go so that you wouldn't feel guilty. Somebody else took the revenge, not you. You know what I mean? Priya had played her part. She was no longer needed. You disapproved of her style and she became depressed. She then started hearing voices in her head. You gave her schizophrenia. Schizophrenics with voices in their heads are suicidal. Your brain wanted Priya to commit suicide. And she did. At least attempted. Your mind couldn't grasp that Priya is your alter. If Priya hurt herself physically, that would hurt you as well. Priya attempted suicide, and you landed up in the hospital with a slit wrist. Forgive me if I am politically incorrect, but this is quite interesting. A person with multiple personalities has an alter who in turn is schizophrenic. That's actually very interesting. But Priya resurfaced when you needed her again, that is, the first time we met. And she must have had memories about how she was saved from an attempted suicide. All hallucinations basically."

"So will you now treat me for schizophrenia as well?" Riya asked.

"That doesn't seem necessary as of now," I replied.

The police still hadn't approached me for my verdict about the case. And I delayed writing my report to them. To be truthful, I didn't know if Riya was suicidal herself. Or was it only the Priya in her mind who was so? And now the discovery of Beena as an alter changed things. Priya's schizophrenia as well. In spite of what I told Riya, I could not be cent percent sure about this case—what was real and what wasn't. I would have to dig deeper. There also remained a slight possibility that Riya or Priya did not attempt suicide. That Riya was wanted dead by someone. But I doubted it would turn out to be true.

In the next session, I asked her if she didn't want to call her parents or office and tell them that you are admitted to a hospital.

"No. Not office. Not now," she said. "I want you to consider this. If I don't go to the office, they will assume I found another job. That would be better, rather than telling them I am undergoing psychotherapy. As far as my parents are concerned, I can wait a few more days till this sorts out. As is you are not going to perform any surgery on me. They are not in the city. So why make them worry? We can decide that later. There isn't a problem with the hospital dues either or is there?"

"No. And our department is not short of beds."

I started with the hypnosis. This time, I wanted to tap into Beena's personality. She was not a dominant personality like Priya as far as Riya's disorder was concerned. I wasn't sure if Beena would be readily accessible to me. So I decided to tap into Priya's personality and then through her, access Beena. I manipulated my way to Priya's memory of the time when Beena took her home. After Priya stopped the video recording in her narration, I thanked her and asked for Beena. I waited for her to answer. And fortunately, she did quite instantly. I asked what made her bring Priya home. She said she wasn't initially aware of Priya being a girl. But now even when she knew it, she was so aroused by her already that she wanted to continue.

"Weren't you thinking of Jay? That you were cheating on him?" I asked.

"I committed to Jay because I feared losing him—losing him to Riya. Isn't it different from being committed to someone without the presence of fear of losing him? Moreover, cheating is only when one finds out about it. I didn't know this girl had her own way of cheating. I realised only later when she sent our videos to Jay that she might already know Jay and me."

"Did you regret it in the morning after the alcohol wore off?"

"Sex? No. Cheating on Jay? Yes. And that too only because Jay found that out through the videos."

"Are you a bisexual then?" I asked more out of curiosity because I wanted to know what she would say, rather than as a part of data that might be useful for Riya's treatment.

"I don't see it that way. This was a one-off. But I would have perhaps continued to have an affair with this girl, maybe under the effect of alcohol or even without it. She was sexy," Beena replied. "I just wish she hadn't done that. What she shared about me made me feel ashamed of myself. Some things are too private to be shared with anyone. She shared my intimate thoughts, and she shared them with my boyfriend. All that embarrassed me to the extreme. Shame and guilt are feelings that the mind generates only when someone who is not supposed to know something, knows it. Isn't that so?"

"I wouldn't disagree," I said.

Since I knew that Beena was also an alter, a thought had kept nagging at me. What if Jay was also an alter? But of all the characters in Riya's story, I had suspected Jay to be the most real. And that made sense. Riya's multiple personality disorder was most likely triggered by Jay's rejection of her. But that didn't mean that Jay couldn't be an alter too. And so I tried. And to my mild astonishment, Jay answered. I asked and he replied. He regretted giving in to the temptation of going out with Riya even when his first preference was Beena. He regretted kissing Riya and giving her hope. He even regretted being Beena's boyfriend, now that she had cheated on him with a lesbian. He now felt inadequate. It would have been bad as is if Beena had cheated on him with another man, but with a woman... He said he had nothing against homosexuality, but it made him feel small and worthless that his heterosexual girlfriend cheated on him with a lesbian. And that made him regret his decision to ditch Riya. She was always a better person than Beena.

I had some doubts regarding why Riya's mind had created Jay and Beena's alters. I could understand the presence of Priya as an alter. She was Riya's protector. But why Jay and Beena? I had a theory, and after talking to both of these alters, I felt I was right. Priya works on Riya's behalf to exact revenge on Jay and Beena. But the pain and regret wouldn't become real unless the couple felt it all. Riya had created the alters to ensure that pain became real to the people she had wished to hurt. Well, Riya didn't directly talk to these two alters the way she did with Priya, and so on a superficial level, she didn't know how Jay and Beena felt, but deep down, all the alters, their memories and their happiness or regrets had only one source and that was Riya's mind. Deep down in her mind, these memories mixed and gave Riya the satisfaction or the closure that she desired. Beena and Jay's alters were created only so that Riya could get joy out of their suffering.

Before I brought Riya out of her trance, I copied the video from the camera to my computer. Then deleting my conversation with Jay, I copied only Beena's part back to the camera. As of now, I didn't want to share it with Riya that there was another personality hiding in her in the form of Jay. The main objective of this session was to ensure that Beena actually was an alter. Priya, the dream-doctor, Beena and now Jay—four alters already. Were there more? Riya's story had these four main characters. But that didn't mean she couldn't have more alters unrelated to this main storyline. Alters may or may not be aware of other alters. In this story too, Jay and Beena's alters didn't know Priya's name though they were aware of her existence. Similarly, there might be other characters or alters who Riya herself didn't know. They might come to the fore under different and unexpected circumstances. I could tap into those only if I knew of their presence. But this was only a possibility—Riya most probably didn't have any more alters. As usual, I showed Riya the video.

"Don't you think," Riya said, "that I am suffering from this disorder for nothing? All this revenge and closure business is only in my mind. Jay and Beena in the real world remain unaffected. If only my mind could understand that..."

I felt bad for Riya. She was right. All for nothing, she thought and I had to agree but I didn't say so.

"This makes for an interesting story," I said. "You have a brilliant mind. What if you write a book on your condition? It has the potential to be a hit—a best-seller. When that happens, you wouldn't have this all-for-nothing feeling."

Riya smiled, perhaps considering my suggestion.

It had only been two days since I had Riya as my patient, but I had got so involved in this case and I had come to know so much about her and her alters that it felt I had known Riya for years. And yet, it was so enigmatic. The feeling that the patient has about what's real and what's imaginary is also shared by her psychiatrist. He has no way of telling if whatever his patient has narrated is indeed the fact, even if the patient is under hypnosis. That is because all the memories that the patient thinks as real may be a result of hallucinations. I had to verify the so-called facts in this case from someone who was not Riya. But I was quite sure this would be only a formality. Even Riya, because she was so intelligent, had already deciphered a lot even before she met me. But the formality had to be done. No loose ends.

I had learnt from our sessions about Riya's childhood too. I had to know that to find out whether there was some childhood trauma or if there was a clue of this condition in her childhood. I had also found out where Riya worked. We both thought Priya was only an imagination. Beena may be too. But Jay was the most real. I had to contact Jay. The next day, I contacted Riya's office and asked the operator to connect me with Jay.

"Yes? This is Jay," I was transferred to Jay's extension.

So Jay did exist! I told him I was a doctor from the psychology department of a government hospital. I told him it was regarding one of his colleagues, and that I would not be able to say much over the phone and requested his presence. Our hospital wasn't far from the place where Riya worked, and I was hopeful Jay would agree to meet. Upon hearing that it was about one of his colleagues, he readily agreed to meet. Half an hour later, he was at the hospital. I was glad that I didn't have to wait to meet him till after his office hours ended. He came in with a young woman. I didn't know who she was. I was reluctant to say anything in front of her. My meeting with Jay was not exactly official.

"She is my colleague from the office," Jay said, perhaps sensing my awkwardness. "I will tell her everything about our conversation. So why not have our conversation in her presence?" he proposed.

"Is she a lawyer or from the Human Resources department?" I asked.

"No, nothing like that," he said and smiled cordially. "She is not just a colleague but also a close friend. By the way, why do you think I agreed so readily to meet you without even asking the details about what it was? That is because I already guessed that when you said you were from the psychology department. Ah, am I wrong...?" Jay asked, doubting his judgement.

"No."

"How is she?"

"She is doing great, given her condition."

"Hope I don't have to meet her."

"No, but you can see her. Come."

Jay looked at her female friend and shrugged.

"She won't be able to see you," I said and gestured towards a door.

Jay cautiously looked through the small circular glass window on the door, taking care Riya wouldn't see him. After him, his female colleague too had a look. Suddenly, they both looked sad.

"Yes," he said. "I thought you had called me about her. Is it clinical depression?"

"More than that."

"I had no idea she was here but when you mentioned the psychology department and said it was about my colleague, I was sure who you were referring to. That's why I quickly came here."

"I appreciate that. Thank you. Let's go to my office," I said.

"This is not exactly official," I said once we settled down. "I needed more information. And I could think of no one else. I may ask you questions which you may find difficult to answer in front of your colleague here."

"No. In fact, I brought her with me because she could also give you more first-hand information."

Who was she? I thought. Riya's friend perhaps. I wouldn't know her name. Or was she Beena? First of all, I wasn't sure Beena existed. If she did exist, would she come? She was supposed to be one of Riya's bullies. Or maybe she wasn't, and only Riya thought she was. I would better ask who this colleague of Jay's was. But that could wait.

"How did you guess about whom I had called you?" I asked.

"She was my friend. I know her nature. I have seen her behave in ways that could warrant seeing a psychiatrist. Moreover, she hasn't reported to work for around a month."

"What?"

"Yes. You didn't know that? How long has she been here?"

"This is the third day," I replied. "And I had thought she was going to her office till the day she was brought here or at least two or three days before that."

Yes, I had actually thought so. I had thought that Riya's alters had surfaced only when she was all alone at the seaside in the evenings. I had assumed she went to her office and work kept her busy during the days. But in the evenings, her inner world haunted her. It was possible that Riya hallucinated only in the evenings when she thought she met Priya. Once Priya left, Riya could return to her normal self.

"No," the woman with Jay spoke for the first time. "When she did not report work, Jay was a bit worried. He called her a couple of times in spite of what had happened between them, but she did not answer his calls. Our office has now assumed her to have absconded. She is no longer our employee."

What's true? What's not? Was Riya's condition older than I had thought it was? Was what I assumed to be true not actually so? I had to listen to what these two had to say to find out. But would they tell the truth? Or would they lie or hide something? Who should I believe? What should I believe and what should I discard? Had Jay known about the suicide, would he have come? But he had come. Did that mean he had no role in the events that led to Riya's slit wrist? Or had he come to clear his name?

"Tell me what happened," I said. "And tell me as if I know nothing. I don't know your side of the story. So only you know where to begin. But you can begin by telling me how you two met. Since how long you have known her."

"We joined our office," Jay started narrating, "around two years back. On the same day. Gradually we became friends. Hmmm... I started to like her more than a friend. And I started suggesting that we go on a date. She didn't refuse outright but she never actually went out with me. After a while, I started to believe that she did not want to be romantically involved with me but couldn't refuse me either maybe because she didn't want to hurt me."

"Wait. Wait. Wait," I said, interrupting Jay. "I thought you were an older employee than her at your office."

"No. We met each other on our very first day at the office. We were assigned to the same team. That's how we became friends."

"Who are you talking about?" I asked.

"Beena," Jay said.

"Ah. Alright. I have heard about Beena. But I thought you would start with Riya. Please carry on."

"You've *heard about* her?" Jay said, astonished.

"Yes, I have heard about Beena," I repeated.

Jay looked at his colleague and she raised her eyebrows.

"There seems to be some confusion or misunderstanding," Jay said. "What is the name of your patient?"

I squinted at him.

"Riya," I replied. "Why?"

Jay looked stumped.

"Do have any identification of hers?" he asked.

"No. She seemed to have lost her purse. Or her purse got stolen. But why do you ask?"

Jay pulled his identity card from his bag and placed it before me. The woman sitting beside him, on his cue, placed hers on the table. I saw Jay's card. It was his office identity card. Then I looked at her card, and I stood up with a start. Her name read Riya. I looked at her photo and again read the name. And still, it read Riya. I looked at her face and then looked back at Jay.

"Is she impersonating me?" the woman in front of me asked.

I slumped down into my chair again.

"She tricked you, doctor. What did she tell you? You were deceived. Right?" Jay said.

"By what name do you know my patient?" I asked Jay.

"Your patient's name is Beena, doctor. Not Riya. My friend here, sitting next to me, is Riya."

"Give me a minute," I said.

"Sure doctor."

I got up and paced up and down behind my chair. I was thinking about all the sessions and conversations I had with Riya, or rather, Beena, over the past two days. Was she trying to deceive me? Trick me? Make a fool out of me? Impersonate Riya? No. Why would she? Beena had a condition. And I had been able to peel away only the surface. At the time I was in sessions with her, I had felt, I had peeled away all the layers. But this was more, much more, complicated than I had thought. I had judged an ocean by its shallow waters at the shore. I sighed, closed my eyes, took a deep breath and sat back in my chair.

"No," I said to both Jay and Riya. "Beena is not trying to trick anyone. Her mind is playing tricks on her. Tell me your story and I will try to explain what's going on."

And so Jay began again.

Jay and Beena—my patient, Beena—became friends. They had joined the office on the same day. And people who join a company on the same day and are placed in the same department usually tend to form a bond. And this was what happened. As days passed, Jay also started getting romantically attracted to Beena. She was very intelligent, beautiful and sexy too. Jay started suggesting sometimes subtly, sometimes more directly that they go out on a date. But Beena kept making excuses and delaying it. Jay, after a couple of weeks, assumed she was not attracted to him and stopped asking her. He even started distancing himself from her. He would find excuses not to go with her for lunch in the office canteen. He would cite work pressure not to accompany her even for evening snacks. And when he started doing that, Beena would stick to him. She would not go for her lunch if he would not go with her. She would miss her evening snacks as well. Seeing this, Jay started being with her again. But again when he would ask her out, she would find excuses not to go on a date with him. Jay mentioned that Beena kept giving him mixed signals. Whenever he tried to distance himself from her, Beena wouldn't let him. And whenever he tried to come close, she maintained distance. Jay reckoned she wanted only friendship with him. Though she didn't want to be romantically involved, she didn't want their friendship to break. Either this or she was indecisive. Maybe she had problems with commitment. So he decided he would continue to be just friends with her. He continued to go with her in the canteen. She became a close friend but just that.

Seven months back, the real Riya sitting in front of me joined the company. She was a simple girl who came here to the city from a small village. Not caring about the trends in fashion, she used to tie her hair in two plaits. She was teased for that. And yes, Beena had indeed been a part of it. Jay did not approve of Beena's attitude and behaviour towards Riya. He even said so to her, but she didn't back off, and he finally let go of the subject for their friendship. A couple of months later, Riya gave up her hairstyle, but the name 'two-plaited-weird girl' had stuck.

Later, Riya and Jay were introduced formally to each other because of a project in their company. She soon realised that Jay behaved normally with her. He didn't care what they called her, and he didn't care if his colleagues would tag him as the weird girl's friend. He was polite with her and what others called her didn't matter. They struck a good rapport and friendship. She started getting attracted to him. Whilst Riya herself narrated this part of the story to me, Jay kept glancing at her, and I could see that he admired her. Riya finally asked Jay out one day but he refused. That was around a month back. Saying that, Riya stopped narrating.

It was Jay's cue to continue.

"When Riya asked me out," Jay narrated, "until that time, I had been sure that I had lost all romantic interest in Beena. But when

Riya asked, I realised that I couldn't go out with her because I still had some feelings for Beena. Somewhere in my mind, I still hoped that one day, we would be together. The next day I told Beena about Riya's asking me out for a date. I told Beena that just as a person would share his life with a friend. Though I still felt something for her, the feelings were not as intense as they had been before. Moreover, I was certain Beena would remain unaffected. And she did remain quite indifferent. She asked what my reply to Riya was. As of then I had refused and I told her that, but I also said that since Riya seemed to be a nice girl and she and I were close friends, my decision might change in the future."

Riya and Jay exchanged glances and smiled at each other.

"Beena nodded," Jay continued, "but remained silent. What happened later was unexpected. Beena went and met Riya. It was a confrontation. She tried to intimidate her. Riya was never to ask me out again, she commanded. If anyone was to be my girlfriend, then it would be her, not Riya."

"I tried to explain it to her," said Riya, "that I didn't know they were together, which actually they were not. But she wouldn't listen. She threatened me with consequences. I didn't know what she meant by consequences, but it was an outright threat. She insulted me and said a weird girl like me did not deserve Jay. I was on the verge of crying but I controlled myself. I didn't want to give her the satisfaction that she had been successful in dominating me. She pointed a finger at me and ordered me to stay away. That I should not go to Jay and tell him anything of this. Or I would face consequences. Again I didn't know what she was talking about. As soon as she left, I met Jay and told him everything. I felt that maybe Jay would take her side given their old friendship, but he did not."

Jay had completely lost his temper on Beena the way she had talked to Riya. He had never approved of Beena's calling Riya names. And she had crossed all limits that day.

"Forget any romantic relationship, you are no longer even my friend," Jay told Beena.

"Yes, why would you be my friend? You've got a girlfriend now," retorted Beena.

"Riya is not my girlfriend. She's not even my best friend. She has nothing to do with it. I would have done this even if it had been some other person. I am breaking our friendship only because of you; you alone are responsible. My patience with you is over."

"No. Wait," Beena said.

"For what?" asked Jay.

"I may have behaved badly and wrongly. But you are my friend."

"No, I am not. Be a better person and find a new friend," Jay said and left.

Beena, Jay said, never returned to the office after that day. After the first two days, Jay called her. Yes, he cared though he no longer wanted to be her friend. But Beena did not answer, and neither did she call back. Beena did not even answer anyone else's calls from the office. After a couple of days more, she was declared as absconding by the company. She was no longer their employee.

"That's all," said Jay. "After that day, we saw her here for the first time. When you called me up, I thought it was about her. But to be truthful, I was also hopeful it would be her because that way, I would at least know she was well even if it meant some psychological issue like depression. She totally vanished from social media too and blocked everyone from our office one month back. I didn't want to visit her or meet her but still wished that she be fine."

"She's fine physically," I said.

"Do you really think she has a condition?" Riya asked. "Is it possible that she is doing it to get Jay's attention?"

"Not impossible but improbable. She slit her wrist. She was not brought here for psychological treatment. There was no use getting Jay's attention after she died."

Riya's jaw dropped, and she covered her mouth with both hands, shocked.

"Beena tried to commit suicide!" Riya exclaimed and Jay gasped.

"Not exactly. Her condition is complex."

"And why is she telling you that she is Riya? Is she trying to implicate me in something?"

"No," I replied. "See, of all the things she has told me, I don't know which are true and which are the ones that only her mind thinks that they are true. So I have a couple of questions. Does she live alone in this city?"

"Yes," replied Jay. "Her parents and sister are settled outside the country. She doesn't want to leave our country. So she stayed back."

"Was she a clever student at school? Do you know anything about that?"

"Yes, she was. From what she told me of her school life, she always ranked first in her class. She thinks that because of that she never made any good friends at school. You might know why."

"Yes," I said. "If you rank first once in a while, all students admire you. The second and third ranks are also admired. But if you are always first in your class, other students tend to start resenting you. The first slot is always occupied. The other students can only guess for the second, third and fourth positions. This takes some of the pleasure out of competitive students. The perennial first-ranker becomes out of reach and a subject of gossip. Children usually don't like him or her. The first-ranker becomes a favourite of the teachers, and again naturally, the others dislike teachers' favourites. Because whatever you do, there is that one person who is always there between you and the teachers. Those first-rankers sometimes also tend to be arrogant."

"True, doctor. I think the same happened with her."

"She grew up in the city, right?"

"Yes. Born here. Schooled and graduated here."

"Riya, you are from a village, right?" I asked. "How were you as a student?"

"Average," replied Riya. "Never reached that first rank."

"Your parents are still there in the village?"

"Yes."

"Who got appreciated at your office for your work—you or Beena?"

"We both did. Sometimes her, sometimes me."

Beena knew about Riya's background. The Riya that Beena thinks she is, is a mixture of Beena herself and the real Riya. The hallucinated memories she has are her own on the backdrop of Riya's life's background. What's real and what's not—Beena doesn't know.

"You didn't tell us," said Riya, "why she is calling herself Riya."

As a doctor, I shouldn't tell them my patient's diagnosis. But if they know about Dissociative Identity Disorder or Multiple Personality Disorder, they will eventually guess.

"Whatever I tell you should remain between the three of us," I said. "I have no other option but to trust you. And you have helped me and in turn, Beena. So ethically, you have the right to know. But I also have the right to trust you. Never break that trust."

Riya and Jay looked at each other.

"We agree," said Jay.

I told them what disorder Beena was suffering from. I told them her story—what she felt was real. I told them a gist of what Beena had told me about the last few days or the last month or so. I told them about her imagined childhood which was a mixture of her own and Riya's life.

"But why me of all people?" asked Riya. "Why me when she has hated me and ridiculed me?"

"It's complicated," I said. "You know people, who laugh not with others but at others, are insecure. They want to fit into a group so that they are not left alone. Beena's childhood was lonely because she was smarter than most kids. She didn't want to be left alone in the office. She laughed at you and ridiculed you. And perhaps most of it was because she wanted to be a part of a group who liked to gossip about you. And maybe in her subconscious mind, she knew what she was doing was wrong. I obviously am not stating this as a fact, but only speculating. Moreover, Jay never approved of her behaviour with you. She liked Jay, even perhaps was in love with him. The more he disapproved, the more she did it, just to prove to Jay that she was right in what she was doing and that you deserved all the ridicule. She hoped that one day Jay would agree with her. As Jay said, Beena was wary of commitment. But that doesn't always mean that the person who doesn't want to commit does not love. She might have fallen in love with Jay, but she stayed away because of her commitment issues. She wanted Jay for herself but without the commitment part. Then you asked him out, and she must have become paranoid—anxious that she might lose Jay permanently to the very person she ridiculed. This insecurity made her confront you, threaten you. You told Jay everything, and he went and broke his friendship with Beena. From what Jay told us, she admitted to being wrong. I am inclined to believe that she said that not just to keep Jay's friendship, but she actually meant it."

"How could such an adamant girl admit to being wrong and really believe it?" said Riya.

"Hear me out," I said. "Jay refused to consider being friends with her. At that moment, she must have felt extremely sad."

"Yes," said Jay. "She did. I could see the pain on her face. I myself felt hurt when I saw the look on her face. I didn't know I was capable of hurting someone so much. And that too, Beena who was my best friend. But I had lost my temper. What she had done, I thought, was not in any way forgivable. And yes, my patience with Beena was over. I could not hurt myself anymore because of her."

"I understand," I said sympathetically. "After Jay broke his friendship with Beena, she must have felt both anger and sorrow. The most difficult emotion to deal with is guilt. Unlike anger, you cannot take it out on anyone else. You cannot hold anyone else responsible for it. That's what guilt is all about. You have only you and your guilty self to deal with. She felt guilty to have ridiculed Riya. Beena felt guilty about not being able to commit to Jay. She felt helpless to have lost Jay as her friend. And all she could do was curse herself for being what she was. That, in the course of a few days, became unbearable. So unbearable that she no longer wanted her to be herself. She did not want herself to be Beena. She wanted to be someone else. And who other than Riya would she want to be? Riya—who like Beena—was perhaps in love with Jay. Riya—who Jay might one day fall in love with. Riya—who Beena had ridiculed and felt guilty about. Riya—whose ear lobes are attached like Beena's own."

At this, Riya touched her ear lobes instinctively while Jay turned and looked at her.

"And then," I said, "Beena flipped. She became the good girl, Riya. And in her story, the antagonist was Beena whom she despised and who she no longer was. You know that's her way of saying sorry to both of you. Especially you, Riya."

A tear rolled down Riya's cheek, and Jay's face looked pale.

"The story doesn't end here," I continued. "Beena exacted revenge on the Beena in her story through an alter of Riya who she called Priya. Riya with a P. The real Beena had been angry with Jay because she broke their bond of friendship. So when Priya avenged Riya, she inadvertently also hurt Jay who broke up with the antagonist Beena. But the real Beena is in love with Jay, and so the alter-Riya in Beena's story does not approve of Priya's method of revenge. Priya then became schizophrenic and tried to kill herself. But since Priya is also Riya who in turn is Beena, she inadvertently ends up slitting her wrist. That's what she was brought here for. A slit wrist. In reality, Jay refused Riya's proposal to go on a date with her. But in Beena's story, he went out with Riya and then ditched her the next day. This again has a reason. The other human emotion that is difficult to handle is rejection. If a person breaks up with his lover on account of someone else he has started liking, it is difficult to accept, but it is still far easier than the feeling of rejection that stems out of the rejection where no other person is involved. Then you start finding fault with yourself just like you do when you feel guilty. And that kind of rejection is worse. The real Jay had told Beena that he was breaking his friendship with her only because of her behaviour—and not because of Riya or anyone else. Beena knew the pain of that rejection. She didn't want the Riya of her story to undergo the same pain. So she brought in alter-Beena who lured

Jay away from her. That way the rejection became easier to bear. After the alter-Riya got her closure, she stopped being in love with Jay. So, in Beena's story, Riya kind of ended up rejecting the person who had rejected her once. Poetic justice, I would say. The alter-Riya, who Beena thinks she is now, ended up being stronger than the weak emotional person that she was earlier."

For a while, none of us said anything. Silence. Then Jay spoke up.

"Is it my mistake? Am I responsible for Beena's condition?"

I chuckled and Jay looked at me, surprised.

"Sorry," I said. "I see guilt. Now you don't start feeling guilty. You know what happened to Beena. No, it's not your fault. If I see anyone's fault, it's Beena's. But she has her own friendless childhood and perhaps her predisposition to this condition to blame. But I don't see her as guilty anymore. She has had her penance."

"It's so complicated," said Riya.

"Yes, it is," I agreed. "Initially I had thought *Riya* had multiple personality disorder, and that too a complicated one. But now, after meeting and talking to you, I should say it is even more complicated. It is *Beena* who has multiple personality disorder. But she has only one alter—Riya. Riya, in turn, has multiple personality disorder. And she has multiple alters—Priya, Jay, Beena and a psychiatrist like me who we call the dream-doctor. Priya who is Riya's main protective alter, in turn has schizophrenia. It's all unsettling from one perspective, but it's beautiful too in a way."

Riya looked at me incredulously. She couldn't believe I found Beena's condition beautiful, but Jay came to my rescue.

"I agree with you, doctor," he said. "It is overwhelming. But it is interesting. The intricacies of Beena's story. The logic. The poetic justice. They say you cannot understand a person till you wear his shoes. And Beena put on many such shoes."

The real Riya shook her head at both of us but smiled.

In my earlier sessions, I had tried to tap into different alters of Beena. But I had done that assuming my patient was Riya. The

Beena who I had summoned during hypnosis was an alter of Riya. Why was I not able to tap into the real Beena? It was perhaps because I summoned Beena after I talked to Priya; so the alter-Beena answered. The real Beena is not at the surface. She's hidden beneath all her alters. The real Beena had alienated herself from her true self. The guilt and the hatred for her own self were so intense that her subconscious had also started believing herself to be Riya. Beena was the villain. She couldn't be her. For my patient to make progress regarding her condition, she would have to remember and accept herself. I would have to peel off the layers but it was going to be a slow process. If she remembered herself in a hurry, she could go back into her shell and bury herself deep beneath one of her alters. I would have to use counselling and hypnosis. During hypnosis, I would have to make a suggestion that my patient remember everything later whatever she said during the trance. It was going to take time.

"Should we meet her?" asked Jay, bringing me out of my thoughts. "Or is it not advisable to do so?"

"No. Don't meet her," I said. "I wouldn't recommend you two seeing her. It might confuse her, or as a defence, she might hallucinate and her brain may create more alters or false memories."

Jay and Riya stood up to leave. I thanked them. Without them, I would have treated the wrong person.

"Will she be OK?" asked Riya.

"I hope there will come a day when you two might be able to meet her. I might need help from you two if I am unable to find the contact details of her family from any other source."

"Yes. We will try to find numbers or addresses from our company database."

"But take care the knowledge about her condition should remain only between us."

"Yes, we will be discreet," said Jay.

After Riya and Jay left, I opened the door to the ward. Beena saw me and smiled. I smiled back. I looked at her for a moment and then waved and left. Entering my office, I sat in my chair and rubbed my temples. The information that Jay and Riya and I had shared with each other was not only overwhelming for them but for me too. The human brain is so complex, I thought. When it goes out of order, it does not in any way become simpler. In fact, in many instances, it becomes more complex. There is a theory in physics that states that when the universe was formed, ours was not the only universe that got created. Many other universes with different physical laws got created. This is a multiverse (multiple universes) theory. Then there is another theory in physics that says that if we have a conscious decision to make, then what really happens is that we take all possible decisions, but one in each universe. Our universe gets split into numerous parallel universes when we make a decision, and one probability is executed in each universe. What if people suffering from multiple personality disorder are kind of special in a way that they have information from different universes about their own selves? What if Beena is Jay in one universe and Riya in another? And maybe, Riya is a lesbian known as Priya in a third universe. In still another universe, she might be a psychiatrist and may be treating a patient who is me. And all this information, Beena in this universe is able to access. She is like a gateway of consciousness between different universes. What if consciousness flows freely between different universes through people like her? Yes, consciousness might have created the universe in the first place. No, not god with small or capital 'g'. The consciousness that created the universe was a primal or crude form of consciousness which pervades every particle in the universe. All conscious beings in the universe may be connected to one another through this consciousness. Maybe this consciousness itself is predisposed to multiple personalities, manifesting itself as a different person through every living organism of each species. If so, people like Beena might show characteristics of all possible conscious persons there might have been under a certain set of initial conditions.

Beena to me is such a type of special person. She is interesting and her mind is beautiful. If the mind of each human being is compared to a sea, then Beena's mind is an ocean. But these are all my own thoughts which may even be far-fetched speculations of an over-enthusiastic psychiatrist. So, I would suppress my curiosity and work on my patient in a more conventional way. Well, there is no other way that I know of yet.

CHAPTER NINETEEN

The Psychiatrist (few years later):

It has been a few years now. I had never had a case like Beena before or after her. I could say I cured her. Well, as far as she could be cured. Her family had come to take her away. But they stayed for a while when I insisted that they give me some time to try and heal her mind. Beena remembered herself, accepted herself, forgave herself and then moved on to another country with her family. But she never wanted to go there and settle down. She takes her medication regularly and has been stable for some years now. I know this because she has stayed in touch with me.

A few days ago, I received a call from an unknown number. I answered it. It was Beena. She said this was her temporary number, and that she was back here in the city for the time being and wanted to meet. And she met me today in the morning. I was in my office when she knocked and came in. I was happy to see her. I smiled.

"Have a seat," I said. "By the way who am I talking to?"

Beena laughed.

"You can make jokes about your patients' conditions. How sick is that?" she said, faking disappointment.

I smiled.

"What brings you here, I mean back to the city? And you came alone?"

"No," she replied. "My alters always give me company wherever I go."

"That was a good one," I said with a chuckle.

"You know, doctor, that I will never settle down in a foreign country. I haven't and won't apply for their citizenship. I will come back here permanently someday. This trip is regarding a movie."

"Movie? What movie?"

"I wrote a book on my condition. You know where I got the idea from? You. You had once told me after you healed me that my case is so interesting that I might one day write a best-seller. Well, I wrote. It's a fiction. Not everything I wrote there is exactly as it happened. And you know, it sold because it was based on a true story."

She smiled.

"I am happy for you. But why didn't you tell me earlier about the book?"

"Because I wanted to meet you and hand you over a copy of it myself," she said and placed an envelope in front of me.

I eagerly removed the cover and looked at the cover page. It had an image of a girl in front of a series of mirrors and each mirror showed her reflection differently. Apt. I smiled.

"Thank you very much. This is lovely," I said.

"Thanks to you, doctor. I wouldn't have found myself again if it weren't for you. By the way, this book sold quite a bit. It's a psychological thriller. Then a few days back, I received a phone from a director of our film industry."

"Oh. Wow."

"Is it not? And he wants to make a film based on my book. That's why I am here."

I looked at her with eyes filled with admiration. She was no longer the antagonist of her own story. She had matured, been the good person that Jay had told her to be and now she was the protagonist. The metamorphosis was complete.

"Are you married or still single?" Beena asked me though she knew the answer.

We had always been in touch, but that was her way of bringing up the subject.

"Who's asking?" I said and laughed.

"Well, it's Priya."

"Priya? But isn't she a lesb…?"

"Sexual orientation is a mindset. Didn't you once tell me that? Priya's mindset has changed. And I think you might find Priya hot, given her history and her dashing personality."

"Shut up," I said with a smile.

"I know. Your ethics and all. And age difference. Well, you are not *that* old, and the age difference is not much. And then think about me. Who would marry a girl with multiple personality disorder? Am I to stay single all my life? Am I to face rejection all my life?"

"Oh wow. Psychology against a psychiatrist?"

Beena laughed.

"Well seriously," she said. "I like you. And you know it, and it's OK that you refuse. It's not going to bring back my alters. I don't take it as a rejection because I know that you will always refuse."

"I don't reject you because of any ethics. I am happy being single. That's all," I said.

"Yes. Yes. You have told me that. But sometimes, I don't buy it."

We had lunch together. And then I wished her luck with her film and promised her I would read her book.

I came back to the hospital and settled back in my office. I liked Beena. Well, not romantically. But sometimes she did tempt me with her attraction for me. I brushed that thought away and started reading a patient's file. But her thoughts kept coming back. She always said I had saved her. Saving is what is done by alters. They are the defence mechanism in a person with multiple personality disorder. I got up and went to the washroom. I looked at my reflection in the mirror. I touched my ears. My ear lobes were free. They had never been attached like Beena's. But since Beena's case, I had intermittently looked at my ear lobes in the reflection. Beena's main alters who were supposed to save her from reality or from her mental condition always had attached ear lobes. I had saved her in a way, but my ear lobes were free. That gave me some relief. It told me I was real. Attached or free earlobes were not the best way to find out, but still, it helped. What's real, what's not?—I sometimes wondered. What if you are not real but just an alter of some other person? How would you know for sure?

Books By The Author

1. echoes in a reflection (Fiction: 2025)
2. Time Loop (Fiction: 2023)
3. Past Present Future (Fiction: Short stories: 2022)
4. Dimension (Fiction: 2022)
5. Surreal (Fiction: Short stories: 2022)
6. Coincident (Fiction: 2022)
7. The Tweak (Fiction: 2022)
8. Day-Twister (Fiction: 2022)
9. Entanglement (Fiction: 2022)
10. The Innervations (Fiction: 2022)
11. 3: 3 Novelettes (Fiction: 3 Stories: 2017)
12. Consciousness Probed (Non-fiction)
13. The Anomalies (Fiction: Short stories)
14. Splinters of Thought (Non-fiction)
15. Spectrum (Fiction: Short stories)